MW01519103

SUGAR
THIEVES

Eric Dupont

SUGAR
THIEVES

A NOVEL TRANSLATED BY SHEILA FISCHMAN

Cormorant Books

Voleurs de sucre copyright © 2004 Les Éditions Marchand de Feuilles
English-language translation copyright © Sheila Fischman, 2012
This edition copyright © Cormorant Books, 2012

No part of this publication may be reproduced, stored in a retrieval system
or transmitted, in any form or by any means, without the prior written consent
of the publisher or a licence from The Canadian Copyright Licensing
Agency (Access Copyright). For an Access Copyright licence,
visit www.accesscopyright.ca or call toll free 1.800.893.5777.

 Canada Council Conseil des Arts   ONTARIO ARTS COUNCIL
for the Arts   du Canada   CONSEIL DES ARTS DE L'ONTARIO

The publisher gratefully acknowledges the support of the Canada Council for the
Arts and the Ontario Arts Council for its publishing program. We acknowledge the
financial support of the Government of Canada through the Canada Book Fund
(CBF) for our publishing activities, and the Government of Ontario through the
Ontario Media Development Corporation, an agency of the Ontario Ministry of
Culture, and the Ontario Book Publishing Tax Credit Program.

We acknowledge the financial collaboration with the Department of Canadian
Heritage through the National Translation Program for Book Publishing.

LIBRARY AND ARCHIVES CANADA CATALOGUING IN PUBLICATION

Dupont, Éric, 1970–

[Voleurs de sucre. English]
Sugar thieves / Éric Dupont ; Sheila Fischman, translator.
Translation of: Voleurs de sucre.
Also issued in electronic format.

ISBN 978-1-897151-81-5

I. Fischman, Sheila II. Title. III. Title: Voleurs de sucre.
English.

PS8607.U66V6413 2012   C843'.6   C2012-902860-6

Cover image and design: Angel Guerra/Archetype
Interior text design: Tannice Goddard/Soul Oasis Networking
Printer: Marquis

Printed and bound in Canada

This book is printed on 100% post-consumer waste recycled paper.

CORMORANT BOOKS INC.
390 Steelcase Road East, Markham, Ontario, L3R 1G2
www.cormorantbooks.com

for Pépé

PROLOGUE

NIXON'S WAR ON DRUGS, declared in the 1970s, was lost, we're told. There was no need to announce the end of the conflict. It is within their parents' sight and knowledge that young people today are rolling their illicit grass. While teachers, beyond their depth, look on helplessly, ever-younger pupils glide, red-eyed, into their classrooms. Never do these hordes of drugged zombies wonder about the progress of the battles that led to this unlimited permissiveness. Ironically, and contrary to all expectations, tribute is never paid to those who've won the war. Instead, emphasis is on the winners of other conflicts at first glance more relevant to the human race, such as World War II or the Korean War. Newspapers laud the vain efforts of the vanquished: governments, parents' associations and police forces. Never, though, are the things rendered unto Caesar that are Caesar's. For good reason: the war on drugs was won by me, and the strategic centre of the battles was not Miami or Washington or Bogota but Amqui, in eastern Canada. At the age of four I was part of the small group that was behind the defeat of the sombre Nixon. From deep in my native Gaspé, I became the hero of a battle now forgotten, but as important in modern history as D-Day or the Battle of the Somme.

Certain factions, however, deny now and forever the need to face facts.

I am four years old, I have just routed my worst enemy in the war for the control of maple syrup, I'm a monster to my neighbour and her vegetable garden, I'm a member in good standing of a biker gang, I have decimated the tribes opposed to the chocolate god and I have a stranglehold on the sugar market in the entire kingdom of Amqui. First a consumer, I'm now on the way to being the biggest supplier in town.

It's the golden age.

I

I HAVE NO MEMORY of arriving in Amqui. The memory lapse
is reciprocal. The town doesn't remember my birth either.
Like Nostradamus's Antichrist, I was born in the Far East.
By that I mean the far east of Canada. The visionary mystic's
exegetes haave always situated in Asia the birth of the Lord
of Darkness, forgetting, in their Eurocentric translations
of some worrisome verses, that everyone is always east of
someone. As far as I'm concerned, that East is called Amqui:
a tiny village of five thousand souls, set like a gem in the
valley of the Matapedia River. As I have no recollection of
arriving here and as I'm too small to ride a bicycle, Amqui is
for me an endless metropolis. Paris and London and Mexico
and even Montreal are not yet real, but mythic places
made up from beginning to end by my father, with the sole

intention of drawing attention to himself. He's fairly good at it, as it happens.

My father is a policeman because he wears a uniform and because his job is to hunt thieves and catch them. Amqui is infested with thieves and he can't do it on his own, even though he spends most of his time on it. From what he says, there must be a nest of them somewhere. I'm already nine months old. Enthroned on my high chair sucking my milk, I listen to him recount his exploits. At first I don't understand why he chose such a dangerous town to bring up his young family. If we're to believe his adventures, the streets aren't safe and his superiors are always asking him to work overtime, probably with the aim of catching another thief who's on the loose. I tell myself that his superiors are well-advised to make my father work. At twenty-two he can still run fast enough to catch the youngest thieves. In my sister's opinion and my own, he'll be senile in a few months. No matter; soon, I've been promised, they're going to teach me to *walk*, and I'll be able to take over from him. Besides, his prolonged absences from the house will allow me to become the king of the household and to take control of the cat, Minou, the dog, Moussette, my mother and my big sister Marie-Josée who, even though she can walk, will not be able to survive on her own in these dangerous lands. I'm nine months old and I hope for just one thing: for the thieves to continue to rule over Amqui to keep my father busy and let me become the Sugar King.

ᘓᕽᓭ

THOUGH I RACK MY brains on books by Hélène Cixous, fall fast asleep over *The Third Sex*, subject myself to endless talks about the three waves of feminism (or is it four?), I'll learn no more about women than what is revealed to me as I sit in my high chair and observe my father, my mother and my sister in this year of grace 1971.

One of their less-known roles is to fatten up little boys who'll get older and one day write about them tall tales devoid of plausibility. There is no exception to this rule. And they are the world's best providers of sugar. My mother is no exception. In her case, she had the political wits to produce her children before she was twenty. Tomorrow's women will invest in their progeny much too late by having them in their thirties. At twenty, my mother still has some trace of credibility. The other mothers in Amqui, full of cravings disguised as solicitude, who file through our apartment, are ancient. Madame Roberge, the neighbour across the way, mother of two brats who'll become brave little soldiers in my army, is already sagging under the weight of years. An upstanding woman, how old could she be? Forty? Forty-five? She must have founded Amqui. My mother is still young and strong enough to be the one who will assure the superiority of sugar in the entire world.

This day, in the spring of 1971, my father makes only a brief foray into the apartment. He leaves almost as soon as he arrives. The thieves won't wait. A moment's inattention and the peace of the town is compromised. So he abandons his role as court jester to run outside and chase a criminal. The table hasn't been cleared and I'm polishing off my lukewarm milk. As Prince of Amqui I am entitled, from my youngest age, to certain considerations. So that later on, when I meet a uniform, whether it's a postman, a customs official or a cop, I'll feel absolutely at home. My father, by the nature of his profession, does not become a fetish. One day I will have to make do with other non-essentials to titillate my perverse inspiration. For me, the uniform will always cover a benevolent father.

2

I SIT ENTHRONED THEN in my high chair, which gives me a fine view of a small part of Amqui. We live in the lower part of a house which, if I understand correctly, doesn't belong to us. The fact that my father has to go running after thieves every day has something to do with it. Later on, when I condescend to start walking, I'll discover that this house is actually a prime lookout post. It sits on a slope, and access to our apartment is at the back. It is flanked by a very green garden and separated from the town by a row of scrawny willows from where you can look down on wonderful Amqui as you like, unseen by anyone. The upstairs neighbours have direct access to rue Saint-Louis, while our door opens onto the garden, which is located a bit below street level. The plateau that is crowned by our residence supports a housing development. Down below, as far as the eye can see, lies the town. Looking up, as our door opens onto the slope and not the street, the plateau ends abruptly after a few streets and makes way for the Matapedia River, which draws around my native plateau an irregular arc.

It's clear that my parents chose this site for its strategic value. From below, nothing and no one can catch us unawares because one of us is always on the lookout. Out back, a ditch several metres deep lets flow the protective river from which Truth will emerge one day, dripping wet. But my story's not there yet.

Compared with the rest of the urbanites, we are privileged to live in a place that's so easy to watch over. Neither the Hohensalzburg Fortress nor the Maginot Line guaranteed Europeans better protection against the invader. One problem, though: from the heart of town a very broad — and if you ask me very poorly maintained — street goes up toward our plateau. For the next three years I'll have to keep a constant eye on a gaping hole my parents didn't anticipate. From the kitchen table I am on the lookout lest some thief who has escaped my father's vigilance is so bold as to climb onto our impregnable plateau. To facilitate my watch and make it more enjoyable, my mother feeds me various kinds of food. My sister, having already been forced to get up onto her two feet, takes over sometimes when I fall asleep.

It is on that day, after my father has left, that my warrior's mission on earth is revealed to me.

"He's crying again!"

"That's because he never gets enough! With you, just one bottle and you were asleep," replied my mother — as if I, the adorable prince, could be content with one paltry portion of lukewarm milk.

"He's already had two bottles!"

"What will we do with your little brother? The upstairs neighbours are going to complain."

෨෬

IT WILL BE A few months until I am able to speak, and that annoying aphasia is starting to get on my nerves. My mother and sister, with no consideration for my handicap, think nothing of discussing my case as though I were deaf. Their disrespect intensifies my rage, which I express with savage howling. My one consolation is the nipple from which the milk emerges, but even that I have to demand vociferously once my bottle is empty. And make it snappy! How dare you let the sentry suffer from malnutrition? A malnourished sentry is liable to do a bad job, and it won't take long for the thieves to climb the brief escarpment that separates us from the town and abduct Minou the cat and Moussette the dog. We'll be in fine shape without those essentials. What a disgrace for the neighbourhood: "Malnourished by mother, policeman's son neglects sentinel duty." The only choice would be exile.

My mother is an expert strategist. She quickly realizes the gravity of the situation and knows that she can't entrust sentry duty to my sister, a walker who doesn't stay in one place and will fail to see the invader's arrival. Besides, in my high chair I'm farther above the ground than she is so the guard's position falls to me. My ribcage is cracked open by my shriller and shriller cries. Angry, I take the spoon that was used to make me swallow some revolting mashed carrots and throw it at the cat, who'll be mad at me for a long time. I don't know how to spare my troops yet. He'll excuse me for my lack of experience.

With a darning needle my mother creates a brilliant invention that would make us millionaires if she were to patent it: she enlarges the hole in my nipple to let through the Pablum she's decided to add to my milk. Before the eyes of my sister, who is filled with wonder at such a clever trick, she gives me the bottle filled with a thick mush of cereal and milk. The enlarged hole does a wonderful job. My mother, genius of the food-processing industry! The warm, thick mixture slides down my throat and calms the unpleasant sensation of emptiness left by the milk after it passes. I empty the whole thing in no time at all, groaning with satisfaction.

Pablum, I will learn much later, is a Canadian invention. Milk has been around forever. No one invented it; but it flows profusely in our house, so well protected from thieves. I click my tongue with satisfaction, which helps my mother feel not so guilty of negligence.

"If he didn't get enough of that, there's a hole in him somewhere!"

The milk-and-Pablum mixture satisfies me for a few minutes, until my appetite, like a malignant tumour, regains the upper hand. I begin again to express my hunger with loud howls that would break an SS officer's heart. This time, my mother has to rack her dietician's brains for a long time before she comes up with another solution to my problem. Actually, it's my father who, unbeknownst to him, has already found a secret weapon to shut me up. He introduced it into the apartment unexpectedly and stowed it in a cupboard at a very lofty altitude. For a long time the can has sat there, awaiting its moment.

On that day the entire world will change thanks to the discovery of that wretched can left behind in the cupboard. I shout myself hoarse, I cry bloody murder, hunger makes my eyes roll in pain, I writhe in my chair like a person possessed while my panic-stricken mother seeks in vain a remedy for my pain, the holy water that will drive away the demon. My sister does what any sister would do in such a case: she takes Minou and Moussette into the garden to shelter them from my ballistic experiments. Between two cries I see my mother, possessed by the spirit of Pandora, open the can that my father brought and set it on the table — after mixing a small amount of its contents to my milk-and-Canadian-Pablum mixture. On the secret weapon someone has painted a log cabin and some big maples like the one that grows in our garden. In red writing I am absolutely and decisively unable to read: PURE MAPLE SYRUP — PRODUCT OF QUEBEC.

Mama seems determined. Lithe and quick, she stirs the golden syrup into the contents of my bottle and holds it out to me hesitantly. Years later, I will see that expression again on the face of a doctor who has just prescribed a revolting cough syrup. The same look that means: "Sorry, can't help it, we've tried everything ... Forgive us." The same resignation in the eyes that I will make out on the faces of American military during a report on the bombing of Hiroshima — those who have been ordered to do the unspeakable. I gulp the medicinal mixture greedily. What I feel cannot be explained save with a metaphor. It is Chartres, the Alps, it is Bernadette Soubirous, Bhopal and Chernobyl, the conquest of the Pole, the Vienna Choirboys on ecstasy, Mozart's Requiem in quadraphonic sound ... I chugalug the bottle under my mother's concern-filled eyes.

Zero hour.

3

AT THIRTEEN I WILL read passionately *I, Christiane F., age 13, Girl of the Streets, Hooker and Junkie*. The book will circulate underground in my school and everyone who matters in the class, meaning most of the girls and two boys, will trade it back and forth in secret for fear that our parents will see what kind of literature we feed on. The book isn't meant for the tender-hearted. Child prostitution, urban decline in Germany, hard drugs: that's all it would take to provoke the censorship committee consisting of my teachers and my parents. It seems to be that the girl who in my mind will be the long-time addiction champion didn't start by shooting up heroin. The hooker in the Bahnhof Zoo followed a very precise junkie's itinerary, the same as what happens to me when I am much younger than she is. When you want to end up in the news with syringes dangling from your arms, you start with grass, coke, ecstasy or glue. My mother has decided that I won't suffer through all those stages in a lucid state by administering the heroin of sugars, the *ne plus ultra* of glucose in its many forms: maple syrup. In the dark history of addiction, the most significant ingredients will be to the very end steadfastly Canadian.

To tell the truth, the poison needs a few minutes to take hold completely in my veins. There's a time of feverish expectation when you wonder what exactly is happening. It takes a second before the drug has effect. First, some pressure in your chest, your soul's urge to leave its shackles. You feel as if you can do anything, you are certain that you'll do everything, but you don't really know where to begin. Significant dilation of pupils. I sense the sugar crystals numbing the tips of my adorably pudgy little fingers. At the same moment I catch sight of Truth for the first time. Just then I'm unaware that that's what it is. I won't recognize her until twenty years later, in a painting by Gérôme; she appears to me totally naked and streaming wet for, as everyone knows, she lives in the Matapedia River. Gérôme depicts her fairly accurately in the body of a woman emerging from a well, armed with her small whip and coming to punish humankind. On that day, grimacing and wet, she whips me right in the face and I fall into a deep sleep, forgetting my responsibilities as watchman. It is my first sugar high and the start of my addiction. It's also the beginning of the end for Nixon, who has just declared war on drugs.

As of today, my head will never be "clear," as Christiane F. would say. You don't get over such toxicities; serious after-effects will go on disturbing me. Sometimes I'll get up in the middle of the night to fix myself a slice of bread and jam. At other times, such as around three in the afternoon, I'll want to sell my last possession for a little maple syrup but have to make do with something else. There is no lasting treatment after a pleasure like that. Just ask people who've stopped smoking: "To the best of your knowledge, have you lost the urge?" Nope. They've stopped performing the act; there's a big difference. So my mother intoxicates me when I'm nine months old. Not wanting to die all alone with my addiction I'll try to contaminate those around me, those who in my opinion are worth the trouble.

4

FOR THREE WEEKS, MY mother serves me the divine brew. In this economy of desire her marginal propensity to import is zero. The secret weapon is made from solely Canadian components: milk, Pablum, maple syrup. Generally she closes the ritual by lighting a tube of herbs, taken from a small cardboard box, that she keeps bringing to her lips to keep it burning and scenting the whole room. The smell of those herbs finishes putting me to sleep after every meal; Truth no longer has to appear and she can go on swimming peacefully in the icy river. Maman seems to have an infinite supply of those tubes of grass that she shares with my father. The substance seems to have magical properties that will allow whoever breathes in the smoke to run faster or to sleep in peace as needed. For a long time I wonder why

Truth appeared only to me and why she waited for my first sugar shock to do so.

Thanks to the sugar's effects I begin to grasp the complex hierarchy that defines relations between men and women. First of all, my father isn't aware of the secret weapon. It's a strategic decision of my mother's. The less he knows about it, the less will thieves be able to learn about us. Informing him would put him pointlessly in danger, at the same time compromising the safety of everyone on the plateau. After all, Germany didn't make a gift to all her soldiers of the plans for the V2 rocket! With the same concern for safety, my mother keeps the secret of her blend to herself and me. Marie-Josée doesn't know any more than the cat or the dog. It's supposed to be a secret forever between my supplier and me. But humiliating circumstances will force her to reveal her secret.

Every time the divine brew is dispensed I take on a little more volume. At the third dose I know that I've reached the point of no return, and that every dose will contain the promise to be as meteoric as the first. The junkie's thinking is very easy to grasp: he is profoundly convinced that he's in perfect control of the situation, even though his poison is administered by others. To fully understand the young junkie's insistence on drugging himself until he touches bottom, his view of those around him has to be presented. He tells himself that they've all been there and that they've managed to get out of it, that he is no different from the adults who simply hide their former dependency behind their reproaches. *I do it for the right reasons* or *The whole world is made up of former junkies* become his slogans.

After three weeks of the secret concoction I begin to swell up in an odd way. I become short of breath and that, I think, is what alerts my father. Though he burns as many tubes of herbs as he can, my breathing is no better. My mother has no choice but to tell him the secret of my silence. He is flabbergasted. Proof that the mixture acts not only on the one who consumes it but also on anyone who learns of its existence. I win a drive in the green Ford station wagon to a place called, brusquely, "Hospital," so that a committee of wise men can study my "case." I dislike that word immediately. Its consonance augurs nothing good. Its consonants are too harsh for my state of clairvoyant consciousness. It's repeated several times, though; as a sentence, it will reverberate in the labyrinth of my ears for a very long time.

The Amqui hospital is located, like Dracula's castle, on the top of a mountain, light years away from our plateau. I am transported there by my father and mother while my sister stays at Madame Roberge's place to stand on guard. When I get there, a horde of men and women clad in white like seagulls bunch together around me, beatific with admiration of my cute little facey. That is where I learn that my mother, though a genius in chemistry, knows nothing about espionage. She explains to them in detail the composition of the elixir of silence with which she has been feeding me for three weeks now, never suspecting that we're in the middle of the enemy camp. I quickly become aware of it when the head seagull, who is called "Doctor" — another violent-sounding word — starts to reveal his game. On all sides I hear "Doctor this," "Doctor that"; a voice from the ceiling shrieks the names of invisible Doctors. Good Lord! Does that mean there's more than one? That word, uncommonly ugly and incredibly violent, is with me when I come down from the magic mixture. Terror makes me vomit.

"For God's sake, what did you give this child?" he asks, feigning total ignorance even though he suspects that he's on the trail of a secret greater than himself. Later on, if he played the torturer in an Anglo-American co-production, they'd have to give him a guttural accent — German, Russian, Arabic or some other scary tone undesirable to the Allied ear.

"Milk," replies my mother.

"Milk? From the look of the child you've injected him with pure tallow!"

"For heaven's sake!"

"I have to know what he ate."

Scientists are like that. Knowing what I had to eat is useless to him for diagnostic purposes; it's fairly obvious that I quite simply ate too much. But they ask you questions like that in the hospital, "to help us help you," as they say. All they want to hear is the next story to tell their wives, their mistresses or their cardiologist colleagues. If you turn up at the ER after swallowing some illicit drug or other, you'll be asked for details, even though the treatment is always the same: an enema. They just want you to serve as an example to the nurses' children, via the medium of their gossip.

"I gave him a little Pablum ..."

"A little Pablum never created such a monster."

"With maple syrup ..."

"Are you out of your mind?" asks the man of science. "That child is liable to die. He has to be hospitalized and put on a diet at once."

Is it useful to note that the big boss in this place of horror would have rendered the same verdict, followed by the same sentence, even if my mother had force-fed me turnip juice? One point to the budding dietician: turnip juice wouldn't have turned me into a miniature Michelin man. A second point to the psychoanalyst: turnip juice would have been identified as a motive for a bloody matricide.

My mother falls into the trap. The Doctor's horrible bluff works and my parents abandon me in the hospital where I am subjected to a good many tortures. It's my first detox experience. I resolve that if I survive this visit to hell I'll learn to talk as fast as possible — even if it means taking lessons from my sister — so I can warn my mother when such vile abuse takes place. Talk and walk: those are my objectives as soon as I'm out of the hospital. Before I have time to build a complete learning program, the effects of my final dose of elixir are beginning to wear off. I decide then to fight with the means at hand.

Years later, I'll watch a report on the American Marines who've come back to the fold after the war in Vietnam. Still in the grip of the amphetamines to which they've become addicted, they beg for their dose. Though no one knows, I am experiencing at this moment, in the hospital in Amqui, the same hell of deprivation.

My own cure is far more violent. Talk with Elton John or Johnny Cash or Marguerite Duras. The Doctor's assistants take turns beside my pallet of torture. I decide to give them their money's worth. For three weeks I howl like a junkie in a state of shock, I spit on the nurses, each one more disgusting than the others. They yell among themselves the word "Nurse" as if it were a military rank: "Nurse Thériault!" "Nurse Desrosiers!" "Nurse Voyer!" They're like unspeakable seagulls that for years will fill my nightmares. There's one in particular I will remember forever. She will appear in my nightmares like a ghost in a white uniform. She demands that the other prisoners call her "Nurse Sirois." They definitely don't skimp on vocabulary in this place. From the painful "Doctor" that is spit at us, we move on to the grating "Nurse Sirois" that hisses above our heads.

She is hopelessly blond and slender, unlike my mother who is a curvaceous brunette. Those are the first signs of her inferiority and her meanness. I think the Doctor concluded a diabolical pact with her because she inherited the perilous assignment of feeding me. Using a metal spoon, she dishes out mashed vegetables specially designed to make me suffer. Carrots, turnips, sweet potatoes and other mashed tubers march past in a little bowl. I believe, though, that I'm giving her a lesson in humility. One day when she comes into my room armed with some slimy yellowish mashed turnips and a bottle filled with skim milk, I don't cry out. Usually I let Nurse Sirois come within a metre of me, and then I start to scream like a stuck pig — in fact, she has chosen the name of that animal for me when talking to her acolytes, though not when my mother is paying me the one daily visit she's permitted. She approaches me then, and I play the game of yielding ground. I put my trust in her. Visibly content, she believes that she's won and I let her stir the purée while giving her my irresistible, angelic look. She smiles her Gorgon's smile and, just as the spoon approaches my mouth, I grab it and throw it in her face. The turnips land right in her eye and she hastens to wipe it off while writhing in pain. What a cow! If this revolting brew seems to be dangerous for your eye and your skin, what would it do to my delicate stomach? I can't believe it; what she makes me ingest every day is so toxic that she's scared about it merely touching her eye. And we get an eyeful when the dreadful woman rinses her eye at the tap. She runs to the corridor. But my victory is of brief duration. Shortly afterwards the wretched woman reappears, flanked by the Doctor.

"So we don't want our turnips?"

"Garghhh!"

I was trying to say: "Fuck off — you and the stupid bitch both, you old nitwit!" But I still have some hard work to do on my accent. He can't make out a word of my insults and forces me to swallow the indescribable gruel while I'm doing my best to kick him. The blonde holds my arms behind my back. The scene is exceptionally ugly, not recommended to sensitive souls.

There will be, however — and it must be mentioned, during those weeks of sequestration as bad as Solzhenitsyn's, as in every concentration camp story — a few rare moments steeped in human kindness. In this hundredth circle of the thousandth circle of hell, which was inaugurated a year before I was born and christened purely out of malice "Hôpital Notre-Dame-de-l'Espérance" (may its fundraisers be plunged in a river of human shit! May its architect be dropped into a scalding grave! May its Board be exposed alive to the beaks of harpies! May the putrid flesh of its decorators be devoured by scrawny bitches!), one of the Nurses, who saw me shut away in my bedroom and who heard in particular my cries of rage, takes an interest in my case. She must have ingeniously infiltrated the hospital as a spy through I don't know what subterfuge. Maybe she's in cahoots with my mother? I'll never know. In the evening, the heaven-sent envoy approaches my bed after the other nurses have left and offers me a gingersnap she's hidden in her pocket. I let her stroke my head and I bite into the divine present. I won't see the mole again for a long time; she's a swarthy little thing who adorns her eyelids with sky blue, probably to display her heavenly origin. My adored Lady of Hope.

The fact that I manage to survive this hospital is proof again that I am destined for battles even more dangerous, and that my hide is tough. Indeed, the weary Doctor lets me leave the hospital, but he forbids my mother to serve me the elixir. That experiment was formative and decisive in forging future alliances. Misfortune makes us grow up more quickly. I'm now ten months old and I've already come to the following conclusions: first, sugar alone makes life bearable. Second, people are divided into two groups — those who give sugar and those who refuse. Third, the latter group includes a very disturbing faction — those who take sugar away from you.

They are the sugar thieves. This testimony is meant as a celebration of their stinging defeat and as a warning for future generations.

5

MY SEQUESTRATION IN THE hospital cracks the solid block
of our family. The first thing I notice is that, in my absence,
thieves still haven't taken over the plateau. My father must
be doing a terrific job of surveillance, and that lets me
concentrate on my new resolutions. My mother's status has
changed, too. She has been placed under high surveillance
and is forbidden to feed me the elixir. She has to use cunning
to pass on secretly the sugar that's become my reason for
living. My sister has been promoted to the rank of official
advisor. After all, she can teach me how to walk and talk, and
she's eighteen months ahead of me in Amqui. She confides
to me that she wasn't born in our town but somewhere else,
where there are other rivers and other cats. I let her yatter
on about those fantasies; I don't ask her to be sensible, only

to introduce me to walking and speech. My training goes on for several months, and I become more and more mobile and voluble. I forgive my father for his disgusting abandonment in the hospital, and I cultivate a relationship with my mother based on trading sugar for adorable smiles.

At this point I must speak about sugar in order to clear up any confusion about its effects, its purity, its nobility. I say this because I know countless imbeciles for whom all sugars are the same. Most of them also march against abortion and urge stricter laws for young offenders. In their hypocrisy, they have a cut-and-dried attitude toward the noble substance that will fuel me for a long time. If I commit the act of simply calling it "sugar" here, it is with the ultimate goal of being understood. Street jargon would be of no use. It is said that Arctic peoples have seven terms for what we ignorant southerners commonly call "snow." The same with sugar. It is a continent to be discovered. There are, first of all, the natural sugars: those found in oranges, plums and raspberries. In the event of extreme withdrawal they provide a meagre substitute thanks to chemical conversion. Beggars can't be choosers. Next come yoghurts, ice creams, soft drinks. They have the advantage of being liquid and of taking effect very quickly. After that comes the first category of controlled substances: candies and pastries of all kinds, caramels, gum, cakes, cream puffs, pies, puddings, etc. With them we are already in the presence of the forbidden. Full, sweet frontal nudity. The boundary between them and what

I'm allowed to ingest is strictly chemical, a matter of concentration. That's all. Finally comes refined sugar, which can have you comatose in a minute. My sister and I don't touch it; it's for real junkies.

But on top of all these forms is maple syrup and its derivatives: taffy, butter and sugar. Aside from maybe honey and molasses, no product is more exquisite, no pleasure more pure than what has been extracted from the maple ever since the Hurons gave away the secret. The recipe is disarmingly simple: just cut a notch into sugar maples and collect their sap, then boil the precious juice over a constant flame until you obtain a syrup. That's all. A simple laboratory can supply plenty of dealers who maintain the high-price glucose habits of their clients. Fortunes and empires have been built around the divine maple leaf. The proof is that all over Amqui floats a red-and-white flag, displaying a maple leaf at its centre. There's one in front of the post office, the town hall, the elementary school and nearly every gas station. The visitor knows as soon as he arrives that he is at the centre of the universe, at the source of all delight.

Now it so happens that even at the very heart of the land of the sacred maple there are ungodly revolutionaries who want to overturn the established order to impose their unhealthy lifestyle — by which I mean mashed turnips and potatoes — on the happy inhabitants of Amqui. Maman is watching, though. Here at our house everyone is required to display a little honesty and candour. Who would exchange three drops of maple syrup for a harvest of turnips freshly extracted from the kingdom of worms, still damp from the earth from which they take their revolting juice? She won't let them have their own way.

My sister and I have just formed an indestructible union. She shows me the essentials: rue Saint-Louis, Madame Roberge's home, Boubou Pizza, the kite-maker and the candy trailer. All the rest — secondary activities not directly linked with sugar such as French, etiquette, reading, writing, school, TV and the opera — I'll happen on later on in life. Another year will pass before Marie-Josée has instilled in me the niceties of walking and talking. Meanwhile, my father keeps hunting thieves and my mother provides me with sugar now and then. But I want more. And then I discover the candy trailer.

In the summer of 1972 my sister gives me to understand that my mother doesn't have a monopoly on sugar, and that if I want to keep up my supply without putting her in a compromising position I have no choice but to venture beyond the garden our kitchen opens onto.

"You can trade bottles for sweets," she tells me one day.

The news affects me like the discovery of penicillin in a Paris brothel.

"Why didn't you tell me before?" I inquire, containing my anger.

"You'd have been out of control. If you promise not to tell Maman I'll take you to the candy trailer."

I have no choice but to submit to her orders. The prospect of gain is definitely too appealing. She takes me then to what will become my Mecca.

The fuss over maple sugar had unfortunate consequences for my mother. Some months earlier, you see, she had started going to the hospital every day to work in their cafeteria. In this way, the Doctor is punishing her with the most severe chastisement that exists. I imagine her peeling turnips from morning till night so the blond Nurse can make other unfortunate prisoners ingest them. But there's another plausible explanation: my mother must have signed up for the gulag of her own free will so she could put maple syrup in the patients' mashed turnips. That's it! Once again I'm dumbfounded by her exceptional military genius. She gets to the heart of the problem. The other Nurse is just a resistance fighter without much power, devoted only to relieving the prisoners' pain. My mother began to sabotage the anti-sugar army most effectively. The thought of being the offspring of such a brilliant strategist fills me with pride even though I have to put up with Valérie, who's been hired to keep an eye on the cat and the dog. They weren't allowed to be alone and, as the cupboards where the cans of cat food are stored are too high for my sister and me, an adult has to spend the day making sure that Minou and Moussette don't lack anything. To us she attaches little importance, having quickly become aware of our autonomy. Even though she has been given clear orders by my father, who's gone over to the anti-sugar side, it's not too hard for her to extract a cake from him in exchange for a little pleading. She does represent a risk though: first of all, she is obsessed with telling my parents in detail what I've eaten, which drives them to reduce even more the already ridiculous doses of sugar I'm allowed. The candy trailer becomes a solution to the crucial matter of stock. For the stratagem to work, though, Valérie mustn't know about our expeditions. On that my sister justifies every theory about heredity using tactics worthy of a Cold War novel.

Valérie has been ordered to put us down for a nap after our noon meal. The window in our bedroom is certainly high, but a clever arrangement of chairs, teddy bears and pillows enables us to reach the sill, open it, and find ourselves trotting along rue Saint-Louis. I follow my guide toward the unknown. At the end of rue Saint-Louis, rue Rodrigue descends to the left on a slope that leads to the city. At the corner of rue Rodrigue and boulevard Saint-Benoît stands the candy trailer, which turns out to be even more attractive than the witch's house in *Hansel and Gretel* — however, it is reassuring to make clear from the outset that no one was ever sequestered or burned alive inside it. Such accusations are just propaganda. It's a trailer covered with sheet metal and flanked by two huge garbage cans twice our height and some wooden picnic tables where strangers consume their noon meal. Often they leave without bothering to throw the soft-drink bottles into the garbage cans.

Now, with no idea how my sister managed to make this discovery, I learn that you can exchange these bottles for sweets. Behind the window of the trailer a brown-haired woman no older than my mother is bustling about; she declares her name is Solange. She is prepared to provide all the sweets we want in exchange for bottles. It's so easy that I'm beginning to suspect it's a trap set by the Doctor. But Solange's eyelids are painted with a thick coat of blue, a clear sign that we can negotiate with confidence. From Solange I learn that sugar has an exact price, and that the plateau's official currency is an empty bottle. With her no need to smile, no need to howl for hours. All she wants is payment, in coin of the realm or empty bottles. The bigger the bottle, the more impressive the pile of sweets given in exchange. Nothing to it. The generosity of those who eat at the tables is boundless. They sometimes quite openly give us a smile along with the bottles we'll take to Solange. The whole exercise lasts no more than twenty minutes, and we often go home with a supply of sweets for at least twenty-four hours, which we hide under a mattress. We've discovered the Klondike. Once again, it's the Doctor who will catch me out.

One expedition day, my mother comes home from the hospital earlier than usual. The Doctor must have got wind of my discovery and orchestrated this hit below the belt from his concentration camp. Maman discovers our exit strategy and yells at poor Valérie at the top of her lungs.

She's totally beside the point. She chews out Moussette and Minou's babysitter for the fact that cars drive along rue Saint-Louis and that we could be squashed by a reckless driver. She must be bluffing. Does she think we're that stupid? We learned how to thread our way between cars ages ago. They actually stop to let us cross, sometimes making a strident sound. I don't understand why she's so upset. Anyway. The time's nearly up for the candy trailer. Marie-Josée practically has to admit defeat. But I must confess that what will really put an end to our excursions to the trailer will be my own oversupply of recklessness.

One day when Valérie is asleep on the sofa Marie-Josée announces an expedition to the trailer. Our supplies are low and I'm really starting to suffer withdrawal. So off we go. At the trailer a very unpleasant surprise is waiting for us: there is no one eating at the tables, no empty bottles on the horizon. Solange is adamant: no bottles, no sugar. My cherubic smiles have no effect on her. She's there for business and we can like it or lump it. Crossing boulevard Saint-Benoît is pointless because we won't know where to go once we reach the other side and, more important, time is passing. Valérie will wake any minute. We have to move fast. While we ponder our plan of attack a noisy group of customers arrives in the parking lot. Straddling metal steeds that make a deafening roar, gaudy, dishevelled individuals make their entrance into the lot.

"Oh my God, it's the Ells!" exclaims Solange.

The creatures are aglow with good health. Tubby and dressed in black, their appearance evokes only strength and courage. With them are women so wonderfully made up that their faces say: "Come, for you I have the rarest and sweetest sugars in the world." Like big hungry bears they gobble mountains of fried things that a trembling Solange has prepared in haste. To wash it all down, the four hairy bears chugalug big bottles of sweet soft drinks. My sister shrinks back and doesn't seem to understand the extent of the miracle: these men are the solution. Simply seeing the richness of the colours that adorn the faces of their companions, one realizes that they're in the right camp and won't hesitate to help two little souls suffering from withdrawal. I go over in detail the strategies that have proved their effectiveness in the past. In exchange for sweets, Solange wants bottles; Maman wants nothing; Madame Roberge wants a nursery rhyme or a sad face; Notre-Dame-de-l'Espérance wants me to touch bottom. What do these new friends want? Their companions, because I'm irresistible, approach me first.

"What do they call you, little pumpkin?"

"They don't."

I've heard one of the Roberge children give that answer and his mother burst out laughing. The laugh earned him a butterscotch pudding.

Laughter like clucking shakes them up. We've won them over.

"Can we have your empty bottles?"

I decide to be direct. I add to my request the pout that sometimes works with Valérie. Widespread laughter and a decisive victory. Marie-Josée and I don't have enough hands to place the bottles on Solange's counter, bottles that my bravura and my vivacity have won us.

We'll go back at noon every day to wait for the angels from hell, and with them we'll sign a secret treaty. The economy of sugar begins a new cycle: these weeks are fat, nearly obese. Becoming the table companion of bikers will be the most profitable collusion of my life. It's as if the gods had come down from Olympus and searched for us actively throughout the whole wide world. And what gods we have! Big solid bodies that the winter wind can try to knock down, goddesses in perpetuity who have all the sugar they want. At this point in my exploration of humanity I place at one pole these magnificent brutes everyone seems to fear, and at the other the Doctor and his Nurses. Between these two extremes sit Maman, Papa, Minou, Moussette, Valérie, Madame Roberge and my big sister. God and Devil. Hitler and Gandhi. The Whore of Babylon and Mother Teresa. That's how we must imagine this opposition. The companions often insist that we sit on their laps. It's a very slim price to pay for such good graces. One noon I sit on the lap of the companion of the man who seems to be the leader of the group because the most buxom of the ladies is reserved for him. My sister is leaning at the end of the table and waiting

impatiently for their ingurgitation to be over. The goddess
decides to chat. I am more willing than my big sister to serve
as the lady's companion.

"What does your papa do?"

"He catches thieves."

"Thieves? What kind of thieves?"

"I don't know. Apparently there are all kinds."

Never has a woman let a child slide off her leg any faster.
The atmosphere turns to lead among the creatures and their
companions.

"Does your papa wear a uniform?"

"Yes, always. Like you, kind of. A policeman uniform."

At that moment three cigarettes come out of nowhere
and are lit.

"Did you talk to your papa about us?"

"Are you kidding? He'd make you stop giving me bottles."

Their smiles come back slowly, as if after a false nuclear
alarm. A smell of adult begins to float in the pure eastern
air.

"If you want more bottles, you know, you mustn't talk
about us to anyone ... Your big sister has to promise too."

"Why?"

She hesitates for a long time before replying, and she looks
at the adipose gods for their approval before describing to
me the nature of their secret mission.

"See, we chase after thieves too ... We have uniforms. Mind
you, they aren't like your papa's, but they're still uniforms.

We do the same thing as the police but in a different way. If the police found out, it could cause a lot of trouble."

My view of the world expands with every word. I imagine new prospects. First of all, my sister and I have been dreaming ever since they arrived of a ride on those remarkable metal steeds.

"We can take you for a spin ... That'll be our secret, too."

She seems to understand the deal. In less time than it takes Solange to transform a bottle into red licorice we're on the steeds that roar in the wind. The creatures drive us all the way around Amqui several times; they drive us along the Matapedia River at insane speeds. We're drunk with power. Not only have we just discovered a secret parallel police force that will keep us in sugar, we are also honorary members of it.

This collusion with the gods of glucose will be a secret for a long time. I'm afraid that my parents will be jealous and will take us away from the world's best dealers. In a few years the reign of my favourite suppliers will be over. We'll make their lives difficult. Other biker gangs will declare war on them, the police won't leave them in peace, unscrupulous prosecutors will work desperately on their fate and have them sentenced to long jail terms on any muddy pretext. Will I be able to pay back what I owe them one day?

⊘⋈⊘

ONE DAY IN THIS summer of 1972, the bikers are smoking (that's the word for the activity that consists of burning the little tubes of fragrant herbs) outside Solange's trailer while they finish their bottles of Pepsi. They seem unconcerned about our presence. We decide to wait, confident they won't forget us. We're very alarmed when they get up abruptly and throw the empty bottles into an enormous garbage container. Total frenzy — how will we get back the indispensable currency? Why are they being such boors with us? Listening to nothing but my courage and the withdrawal that's liable to attack at any moment, I climb the high wall of the dumpster with all kinds of grunting and groaning while Marie-Josée watches, stunned.

"You'll fall in, idiot!"

"Hold on to my feet and don't let go! As soon as I've got the bottles pull me up ..."

"You fat lump — do you know much you weigh? I'll never make it!"

"Try!"

The inevitable happens: my shoe stays in Marie-Josée's hands and she starts to howl. From the bottom of the steel container I hear her cry for help.

"My brother's in the garbage can! He fell in! Help me! Help!"

Solange doesn't budge. She's not going to risk losing a sale by leaving her counter to rescue a poor junkie from the bottom of the garbage can. My cries reverberate against the metal walls of my fetid prison. There comes a moment in the life of every junkie when he touches bottom in a figurative way. The dark and slimy place of dependency, as described by certain American preachers, I have the good fortune to sink my baby teeth into at the age of two. At the bottom of that garbage can are a dozen bottles. I decide to stick my ten little fingers into them. If I get out of here alive, I tell myself, it will be the deal of the century at Solange's place. I feel a powerful hand grab my foot. My sister's pathetic sobs calm down, replaced by hollow laughter. It's an angel from hell who saves me from certain death in a garbage truck. He decides that the course to follow is laughter. I dare to yell at him. My plunge into refuse is very fruitful: I leave with a bottle hanging from the tip of every finger. Solange, clearly impressed by my miraculous catch, adds to her usual amount. We go home with our hands full of candies, which is the final act in my downfall.

ᘒᕲ

I WILL FIND OUT much later what Solange meant by her hesitant phonetic grid "Les Ells!" She means Hells Angels, Angels from Hell, Devil's Henchmen, Disciples of Evil, and so forth. I must admit that, at the time, the Angels don't seem to be an immediate threat; my sugar level is dropping by the minute and nothing else matters to me. Bikers bring salvation.

We've found an unassailable hiding place for all the sugar

we've found here and there: the space under the mattress. But after the incident of the garbage can the spot becomes too tight. Valérie sticks her nose in and forces Marie-Josée to make a full confession: the daily excursions to the trailer, the Angels from Hell, Solange, the full catastrophe! From that day on we will be placed under close surveillance, along with Minou and Moussette, and our world will be delimited by the garden overlooking Amqui and rue Saint-Louis. But as a wise man of our land should have put it: if you can't look for candy, let the candy come to you.

The sorry incident of the garbage can put an end to our stocking up at Solange's. Strangely enough, Valérie stops coming to replace Maman on weekdays. The hospital management must have learned about her strategy; once again she's with us every day. In the fall a horde of thieves must have swept through the whole valley because only rarely does my father put in an appearance at home. Marie-Josée has found other spare time activities with the neighbours across rue Saint-Louis, and I see myself being forced to live in near total isolation. Maman must have realized that my dependency was taking on alarming proportions and chooses to change my diet before I am rehabilitated by the Doctor. She only rarely provides me with elixir, choosing instead less pure and less noble forms of sugar. I'll be going through a rather difficult weaning period without the help of Truth or Minou and Moussette.

Maman sentences me to play in the garden, from where

I can observe the town and its activity from the foot of an extravagant maple tree to which the autumn has given glorious colours. Before my eyes, the noble plant slowly adorns itself with yellow, red and orange. I spend many happy hours observing it in the company of Truth who, probably out of pity, is visiting me more and more often. She always appears when I'm alone in the garden observing Minou perched on a birdhouse. He waits there for his prey, and I watch intently for the bird to emerge from its little house and be grabbed by murderous claws. It is during that horror story worthy of Edgar Allan Poe that Truth comes to visit. She always arrives naked and dripping, as she was on the day when she slapped me for the first time and made me aware of her existence. To anyone else she'd be scary: her long black hair is streaming wet and her coal-black eyes have a permanent look of terror. Her faded skin recalls that of the drowned when they are taken from the sea in spring, and who inspired Zola to lay down the stones of his putrid literature. No, she's not a beautiful sight. When she sits close to me, she places the small whip she always carries on these outings in easy reach in case she finds some blind man to be wakened from his lethargy along the way. Our conversations start to seem like exchanges between a philosophy master and his student.

"Is Minou a thief?"

"Hardly."

"Moussette?"

"Neither. Where do you get such outlandish ideas?"

"Papa often runs after them!"

"The only thieves are sugar thieves. As cats and dogs don't eat sugar, only birds and meatballs, they aren't thieves. If your father chases them it's just to stay in shape for catching real ones."

๏๛

IN THE FALL OF 1972, while other Canadians are preparing for outrageously expensive Olympic Games or referendums doomed to fail, Truth helps me reveal the truth about certain of life's great mysteries. The conversations are intense. As the years go by, like a classmate whom we gradually lose sight of because of the vicissitudes of life, Truth will space out her visits, probably thinking that I no longer need our invaluable alliance.

That weaning, that second detox cure, is imposed on me then by my mother herself. The using of a substance as strong as sugar doesn't stop overnight. For a real junkie, overnight means centuries. In the hospital, what helps you or constrains you is the army of white lab coats lying in wait for you. Doing it yourself at home to avoid a hospital stay is quite an exploit: you set a date, even an hour, for your last dose. You reach a tacit agreement with the supplier. You know enough to dread the horrors to come. Once the effects of the last dose of sugar have been dissipated, it's absolute hell. First your pupils dilate, then you get goose-pimples, and you know the next hours will be atrocious.

"Give me a little!"

"No!"

"Just a bit!"

"I said no."

Cries, tears.

Often the supplier's refusal gives way to uncontrollable acts of violence. Striking out with feet and fists at anything that moves or doesn't. No words can assuage the fire that goes up and up, demanding the white powder. Then you start to search. Could I have hidden a dose somewhere? Could I have forgotten it there? Certainly. It seems to me that just a little would help me get through this horror. Everywhere, closed cupboards, empty jars, packages, hidden cookies. I know that she hides them there, I can sense it. After that your head feels like it's being crushed. By which I mean a horrendous pressure, as if you've been placed in a vise and an invisible hand were tightening it, slowly. Hallucinations: you see clouds of unknown insects, white spots, spiders and communists all over. I roll on the ground; I ask, I demand, I am ripe for exorcism.

Next comes a period of sweating when the body no longer knows if it's a volcano or a glacier. Noisy vomiting. At this point in my suffering I may bite into the big maple tree in the garden in the hope that its sap will relieve my pain. I would say yes to any junk food at any price. Twenty bottles for a jujube? Yes, I'll find them right away or I'll owe you — just give me one jujube, I beseech you! We would sell our cat, slice a finger with a butter knife, for one dried-out licorice. Some inexperienced ignoramuses think they can "sleep off" their purge. Wrong. Sleep would be a liberation, a respite. Depending on the sugar level, that process can last for a few hours or up to three days. And for days, weeks, the irritability followed by sorrow as profound as the Mindanao Deep. Eyes wild, inability to concentrate — is it night or day? The period of sobriety that concludes the process arrives like a balm on a purulent wound.

We know we've come through when we can touch thumb and forefinger and it doesn't feel like a burn. We know too, by the sadness and the urge to start over more slowly, to not let ourselves be had this time, to control sugar and not the reverse. Ambitious pilgrims on the road paved with good intentions plan strange ways of breaking our habit. According to them, you just have to space the doses increasingly far apart. A dose at noon, another at one o'clock, another at three and another at six. A whole lot of good that'll do them. My effort has the opposite effect: the doses come closer together. Noon, one o'clock, one thirty, one forty, etc., and what the hell.

It's at this stage that Chopin's nocturnes become a guaranteed passport for suicide. You need to be surrounded by people.

☙❧

DURING MY MANY TRIES at kicking the habit, I've had the extraordinary luck to be able to take refuge with Minou and Moussette. Whenever Maman or another supplier refuses to give me sugar, those gallant creatures are always there to keep me company. They have the tremendous plus of not speaking. Others try to console me with words they think are soothing: "Come on, you can do without," or the oft-heard "I know how hard it is." Like hell you do! You know nothing about it! Less than nothing! If you know, why aren't you, too, racked with convulsions? Minou and Moussette are a presence, a form of zootherapy more powerful than the methadone for heroin addicts. I sometimes hug one of them tight; the animals seem to absorb all the bad vibes emanating from my little body. Never do they complain, never do they run away, always they come back. Loyalty that would make of Romeo and Juliet inconstant lovers. Madama Butterfly? A woman of easy virtue. Penelope? A libertine. Minou and Moussette: wildlife in aid of a human overtaken by his chemical creations.

During periods of sobriety I suffer in silence, knowing full well that any new abuse would take me straight to the hell of the hospital and the claws of the Doctor and his cruel stepmothers.

It is in front of a maple tree on which a cat is perched that Truth teaches me the art of contemplation while perfecting one's way of speaking. Several spirits haunted by ancestral conflict will ask me in a strange voice, "What is the language of Truth?" The question doesn't even cross my mind until the day when my mother puts me on the trail of a problem bigger than me. According to her there are people kilometres away from Amqui, people who wouldn't understand us because they speak English. That utterance strikes me as strange, to say the least. I want to learn more from my naked nymph of the Matapedia.

"Maman speaks English?"

"No. Your father, your sister, the Doctor, Solange — everyone who lives here only understands French."

"What is English?"

"A tongue; that is, a language."

I stick out my own tongue with a quizzical look. As is her habit, she doesn't laugh. I think that's what I like about her most. She doesn't laugh at my questions the way Solange, Maman, Papa and Madame Roberge do.

"No. A language is a way of speaking, a group of words and sounds. If you spoke to someone who doesn't speak French, they wouldn't understand you."

"Or Maman?"

"I'll let you complete the reasoning."

It will take me several years to get over that revelation. So all over the world there are creatures for whom it's impossible to understand Maman, Marie-Josée and me. Papa must speak English — it's impossible that any important voice is forbidden to him. Truth claims that rare are those who could understand us.

"Yes, but ... how do they understand each other?"

"They understand among themselves, they share the same language."

"Or the same curse!"

"You'll have to learn to see things differently."

"But what happened to them?"

"It's a state of affairs we can't do anything about. Try to be sober for a few weeks and don't worry about the troubles of strangers."

"If I've got it right, it's impossible for those poor voiceless individuals to do without maple syrup. They must need it terribly to get over their sadness at not speaking French."

"Most of them haven't got maple syrup and the vast majority of humankind has never seen it. Its absence doesn't matter to them at all."

My jaw dropped at her cold account of such atrocious suffering. How can she spout these revelations without dissolving in tears? Why so much pain? How can she, without the slightest trace of self-censorship, spit out such crude stories? I think to myself that she wears her name well, and I rush to Maman, sobbing, plugging my ears like a novice who has just been told a joke that's too ribald. Tears often win me a little sugar, a trace of glucose to calm my nerves.

"You are dangerously sensitive. You'll have to get used to some far worse truths."

"I've had enough for today. Please, since you know how

fragile my nerves are, spare me the sensational revelations."

"You'll have to get used to much worse ..."

"Thanks. That's encouraging!"

"I'm trying to help you. I'll come back another day when you've digested this news."

I decide on that day that my life will have no meaning 'til I've managed to console those wretched of the earth for their profound despair. I will become a teacher of French.

ᘒᘔ

MOST OF THE TIME, I'm alone in the garden looking for worms, jumping in the leaves and running after Moussette. By winter, my detox is nearly complete and I experience a very formative Lent: I learn how to walk in the snow, how to use it to make projectiles to throw at my sister, how to lose my mitts and how to tie my boots.

One February morning we find Minou at the peak of despair and the top of a wooden post. He must have tried to catch a bird and spent the night imprisoned there. He can't get down. The poor animal produces meows full of fear and sorrow. I'm the one who discovers him on his perch in the wee small hours; Papa has already left the house and Maman is still wandering around in her housecoat. I take her outside, giving her barely enough time to pull on her boots. The incident gives my mother a chance to teach me what firemen are for: they are men who go around in uniform, but instead of hunting thieves their job is to help get cats down from poles they've climbed too hastily. Their uniform is made of a very thick fabric because when they catch the poor cat the animal is in such a state of crisis that he'll sometimes scratch his rescuer. The fireman uses a big ladder to retrieve the tomcat. Maman in her housecoat and I supervise his work from below. Twenty times the fireman is about to smash his skull on the icy ground, the post is that slippery. His job is worthy of a scene in *Mission: Impossible*. His task accomplished, the fireman goes back to his big red truck. There must be lots of foolhardy cats stuck at the tops of poles in Amqui because he declines my mother's invitation for a coffee.

Intending to educate him, I tell my father about poor Minou's misadventure and how he was saved. I discover that an age-old rivalry tears firemen and policemen apart from each other. Using rudimentary associative reasoning, I tell myself that all men in uniform must necessarily get along; my father shows me that's not necessarily so.

"You called the firemen for that?" he accuses my mother, obviously nettled.

"What am I supposed to do? Leave him up there to starve?"

"You could have waited for me to come home!"

"And how would you have got up there?" Maman has an argument that carries weight.

✆

I DON'T UNDERSTAND MY father's reproaches. Let each man ply his own trade and the cats will survive! Thieves to the cops, cats to the firemen! A good allotment of resources would ensure a certain stability in the world of work. Maman helps me to develop an exemplary trade-union conscience. It's no exaggeration to say that Rosa Luxemburg would have seen her as an example of proletarian solidarity. My mother is practical, my father isn't. In fact, her aptitudes are far superior to everyone else's. She proves it on many occasions — in particular when she's driving the car. She wastes no time waiting for others to slow down or for the driver at the other corner of the intersection to pass her.

"Move it!"

The imprecation stops traffic and lets us move on before everyone else. Her turns are for us brief but intense delights. She makes a ninety-degree turn, allowing centrifugal force to play with us on the back seat like socks in a washing machine. We love going out with her.

When spring arrives, my addiction to sugar is perfectly under control. Maman has done a job worthy of a news report and put me back on the right path. The small doses that I still need to stay alive come only from her. But my troubles aren't over.

In the spring of 1973 I experience another disgraceful relapse. The guilty party is once again my sister, who has kept working in secret, hunting down doses all over the place without a word to anyone.

"Don't you use anymore?"

"Hardly."

"What would you say to a caramel?"

One miserable caramel can't do any harm. I overesti-
mate my strength. Soon I'm at the point I was at a year
ago, but this time with the shame of depending on my sister.
Later it will seem to me that I should have been mad at my
mother and sister. Everyone will tell you though that in this
battle, reproaches are pointless. When you point a finger at
someone, you're pointing four at yourself. I learn that my
sister has discovered a source of sugar even more generous
than Solange's trailer.

Our neighbour, Madame Roberge, has two children and
she stuffs them every day with cakes and jellies sweeter than
the nectar of Olympus. Marie-Josée hit it off with the two
brats ages ago and since then has been in their generous
mother's good graces. I fall then into a sugary spiral at the
centre of which reigns Madame Roberge. We need only claim
to be visiting two children of our age and we can enter the
den of our new supplier. Once again I feel as if I'm leaving
Maman in the lurch in this ethical dilemma. I am beginning to understand that she controls my absorption of sugar
for my own good, but she has initiated me into pleasures
too exquisite to be given up. If I had few scruples about
accepting Solange's transactions, the exchange with Madame
Roberge is much like my understanding with Maman for me
to plunge headfirst without thinking. Chemistry ultimately

wins out over these considerations. In light of the trailer as instrument of exchange, I sacrifice freedom of thought.

With Madame Roberge, matters take on an ease that's nearly unsettling. We just have to keep company with her offspring to obtain cakes and jam.

"It's a little too easy, Marie-Jo. I think she'll want something from us afterwards."

"Don't get your diaper in a knot. She gives without counting and she doesn't rat on anybody."

"If I understand rightly, she doesn't want bottles. We aren't her children and she'll give us secretly all the white powder we want."

"Pretty much. Her children are already hooked on death, but we mustn't talk about that."

The deal unfurls as my big sister predicted. Indeed, the kind lady stuffs us with glucose whenever we visit and we don't even need to drop subtle hints such as "I'm hungry," or "You're very elegant today, Madame Roberge." We just have to step inside her front door and the benefactress lays out the goods. I continue to fear that some day she'll throw a steep bill in our faces, covering the doses not paid for, and that for the rest of our lives Marie-Josée and I will have to find enough bottles to pay her back. Never has anyone asked us for the slightest payment. It's obviously too good to last. Maman is beginning to wonder about the frequency of our visits to the kind lady, and one day the generous neighbour becomes delirious.

"Your maman asked me not to give you so many sweets."

So she had to confess the truth.

"No cake today?"

"I'll give you a little piece but small children should get their sweets from their own mamans. I'm just the neighbour."

Madame Roberge will remain a supplier "in case of emergency," but after that exchange I won't be able to squeeze enough out of her to satisfy my appetite. The situation illustrates behaviour typical of those who give away sugar: first they make you dependent, but they don't like to have competition. They create a monster, then forbid him to eat anywhere else. I think the exchanges with Solange didn't worry Maman precisely because the bottle swap seemed to doom the relationship to strictly mercantile ends. She wasn't at all uncomfortable, and she didn't hold it against the gallant Solange. She seems more preoccupied by Madame Roberge, though. I often ask Truth to give them both a slap, but she refuses categorically every time.

Sitting on the grass with her, I beseech her to come to my aid.

"You're asking the impossible."

"But just one intervention by you would sort out many things."

"You're becoming far too dependent on those women. You have to learn to find what you're lacking somewhere else."

"Where?"

"You'll have to explore. Go out now and then."

"I'd like to see you in my shoes. Ever since the trailer and the Angels we've been kept here like dangerous criminals."

"You disappoint me. I ought to send my sister Liberty to lecture to you but she's too busy laughing her head off in Vietnam."

"They speak French in Vietnam?"

"You're hopeless. My sister doesn't care about linguistic barriers. She's in demand all over the world."

"How does a person get to meet this traveller?"

"Go out."

"You mean go back to the trailer so Solange can rat on me to Maman again? That reeks of hospital."

Her only reply is to jerk her chin in the direction of the lower part of town and disappear into the landscape.

∽

THERE EXIST IN THE world of psychotherapy as many strategies and schools as there are therapists. Since Freud and Jung, packs of charitable souls prepared to help out in exchange for a mere BMW have been fighting over the neurotics, the addicts, the intensely moronic and the melancholic of this world, promising them more or less long-lasting cures, depending on the quality of their insurance programs or their bank accounts. My favourite schools are those whose patients are exempt from guilt as of the beginning of therapy, so that after each encounter in the muffled office they have a feeling of soothing lightness. I avoid the boring kind who remind the patient that he is responsible for his own misfortune and that others are of only secondary importance. Those patients won't last long, whether in Vienna or New York, and are usually recycled onto police forces or the bench.

Had they been able to study my case, all those kind therapists would have pointed to my big sister who, every time I seem to get the upper hand, grabs my foot to drag me deep down into vice. Once again, that's what happens. "Go out," Truth said. I have just those two words in my mind. Once again, I think to myself, I would have to have come in if I wanted to respect the logic of Truth's reasoning. According to my sister, though, you have to go out before you can come in. This piece of nonsense makes me giddy.

"We have to go out."

"Where to?"

"I don't know. Have you ever gone out?"

"Does the trailer count?"

"Maybe ..."

"Take me out."

Marie-Josée seems perplexed. Though usually I resist her temptations, I'm asking her now to take me out. The very word seems surrounded by a halo of prohibition. She thinks it over for a few seconds and then, as usual, finds a solution that will drag us both into an unfortunate adventure. How is it that, of all my advisors, ministers and éminences grises,

I've chosen the one who always takes me closer to my ruin? She has managed in a few seconds to concoct a plan worthy of the Red Brigades.

"Okay, I'll take you out."

"Where to?"

"Don't you remember? Where Papa took us the other day."

"I swear I don't."

To tell you the truth, I do have a vague memory of the place because they gave me a cola whose sweetness was perfect for a one-year-old.

"You were too little."

I don't see what she's referring to; I have memories that predate hers. It seems to me, for a moment, that she is taking us on a crusade to find an illusory Grail brimful of pudding.

"We went with Papa," she goes on, overexcited. "It's really easy, we just have to walk along the boulevard and in a few minutes we're there. You just have to follow me!"

Her plan is disarmingly simple. But, like two amnesiacs, we forgot that we'd travelled the distance in my father's Ford, not on foot. That detail doesn't cross our minds any more than the fact that we have to ask permission before we venture onto the sidewalks along a national highway where trucks go, loaded with wood, metals and other raw materials. So we set out, careful to tell the cat to let Maman know if we aren't back by suppertime. We mustn't be irresponsible!

☾✺☽

COMPARED WITH CROSSING BOULEVARD Saint-Benoît, the peregrinations of Moses are a Sunday stroll. The stream of cars along this road is as dense as Niagara Falls, but not noisy enough to frighten two youngsters aged three and four. We decide, like the explorers who discovered our continent, simply to hurl ourselves into the traffic. We know the word "brake" and its verbal inflections. Car drivers, though, seem to share that knowledge. The people of Amqui celebrate our first outing with loud cries and blaring horns; the marriage procession of Charles and Diana won't be acclaimed more fervently, although we do have the decency to not stop for autographs. Still, these people have good manners, and they seem to respect our anonymity as we are no longer bothered along the way.

Marie-Josée proves to have an uncommonly fine memory and sense of direction. We cross the bridge over the Matapedia while passersby and drivers look on, baffled, as they drive past at breakneck speed. Occasionally I step off the sidewalk to get a better view of the road we still have to travel. Truck drivers greet me with groans of joy and take big detours so they won't throw any dust on us.

"Good God," they howl, making me blush with fake humility.

I go around barefoot, in my most elegant disposable diaper, while Marie-Josée has donned her ceremonial garments: a little blue summer dress with a white tulip on the front. We stroll along with a haughty stride in a town we know only by sight. Right now Truth appears to me as a wise counsellor, though I don't understand how this expedition will help us locate a new source of sugar. I trust the supreme authority of my big sister, who serves as guru in the absence of Truth. We walk past the police station, in front of which a maple leaf hangs proudly — a sign that even our father, recalcitrant to sugar, must in one way or another recognize its superiority.

We walk for what seems like hours. Suddenly Marie-Josée stops me to tell me that our crusade has achieved its goal. Like Champollion facing his first hieroglyphics, we are standing outside the place, unable to decipher the black writing. We must anchor our understanding to extratextual signs. It can be nothing else. We go in without knocking, as if the place belonged to us. Inside, the sanctuary is practically deserted. The smell of frying and tomatoes assails us like a salty wind. The door closes, making the crystalline sound of a little bell. A pretty young brunette emerges from between two double doors and studies us with the same look that Penelope must have reserved for Ulysses when she recognized him. Her amazement is easy to understand: my sister, decked out like a princess, and I, clad simply in my disposable diaper, must make her feel ashamed, as she has on only a drab, stained uniform. My sister guides me while she looks, stupefied, in the direction of one of the empty tables, like an habitué of the spot. She casually looks at a sheet of cardboard held out to her by the guardian of the place, whose expression has gone from one of surprise to a smile. Our charm has won her over.

"You don't know how to read."

"I do so!"

"Oh yes? What does it say?"

"Pizza with mushrooms! Pepsi-Cola! Vanilla pudding!"

My sister has definitely chosen to kill me with stupor today. Not only does she know the best places in town — though she has never left the plateau without Maman — but she has also learned to read in secret. The vestal virgin comes back. We notice that her eyes have a generous coating of blue; we've really ended up with the right one.

"What can I bring you?"

"Pizza all dressed for me and a vanilla pudding for my little brother. Thank you."

Behind the counter, the rest of the occupants shoot us looks that I'll never be able to explain. A friend whose name I will not divulge — a waiter in a Paris café — will tell me that Catherine Deneuve showed up one day without warning. I imagine that the cook and the other waitress are giving us looks similar to those given to the French movie star on that day. My sister's orders are executed promptly. The pudding helps me get over the fatigue of the expedition.

"Any empty bottles?"

"No. What for?"

"To pay, dummy! She doesn't even know us! Do you think she'll give us the pizza and the pudding?"

"Don't worry. I've got more than one trick up my sleeve."

As if she has heard us, the priestess — who is now displaying a nearly unsettling smile — comes back to our table. She hands us a scrap of paper on which she has just jotted something.

"That will be five dollars and fifty cents, my friends."

This part of town has adopted another currency. We can't pay with bottles. Problem.

Post-nuclear silence. I let my sister negotiate with the paint-daubed prophetess.

"But Madame, we haven't even got ten cents!" Laughter, agricultural and coarse, issuing from all the mouths that now surround us. We decide to laugh along.

"What are your names, children?"

"Eric and Marie-Josée."

"Thanks a lot!"

She disappears behind the counter to talk to the Manitou of the sanctuary. He then talks on the telephone for a good half-minute. We are analyzing their odd behaviour and attributing their impertinent questions to overwork when, to our great pleasure, who should come in through the gate of the temple but Papa. He too starts to laugh like a lunatic. Never, I think, have we seen him so happy. What a coincidence! In this vast, sprawling city he shows up in this place where sugar is worshipped! He must be on the trail of a thief because he is wearing his uniform and a police car is parked outside the door. He doesn't even take the time to order and decides to take us home.

ଔଚ

MEANWHILE, BACK AT THE house, Maman has noticed our absence. She and Madame Roberge have looked all over for us. Years later I will feel pretty much the same sensations they do now, but on other occasions: while abroad, trying to find my lost passport; while picking up the pieces of a priceless crystal vase; while awaiting the results of a blood test at my doctor's; while thinking about the matter of collective responsibility for the genocide in Rwanda — in short, the kind of situation that is conjugated only in the past conditional.

ଔଚ

BACK AT THE RESTAURANT, my father's arrival sets off the mirth of the cook and the waitresses. They fraternize very quickly, enough so that Papa gives them little papers as signs of friendship. A ride in the police car awaits us. I think to myself that, right now, Hells Angels, firemen and police are the most useful people on earth, and that a meeting of the three should be arranged so that bonds of friendship can be created. My karma is becoming clear. My sister discourages me from talking to Papa about my plans for a festival of brotherhood. She seems preoccupied, while I'm as happy as twenty popes out on the town; the sugar in the pudding has me as high as a kite. We cross Amqui again with Papa, who seems unable to stop laughing his head off. So some day when I see pornography or a moustachioed man in a uniform trying to look threatening to excite the audience, I'll be as cold as a Little Sister of the Poor. It won't work. The sugar helps me appreciate some very enjoyable and rhythmical music on the car radio that fills the space. I don't understand a word they're saying.

"Who's singing, Papa? You?"

More laughter.

"No, it's the Bittèlzes. They sing in English."

He could just as well have told me it was God the Father or Saint Francis of Assisi. Obviously, I lack a few references. I start listening very attentively to the melody sung by those poor sugar-deprived souls, which must be an ode to sorrow.

The welcome we get at home leaves me mute with astonishment. My mother is stretched out on the living room sofa, practically unconscious, and a tearful Madame Roberge is trying to comfort her.

"Here they are, Madame Dupont! Your husband and your little ones! They're here!"

I'll never forget what I learned just then: that you can slip from the most extreme grief into divine fury. Maman's face goes from an arctic distress to a volcanic eruption. A movement, accelerated a thousandfold, from Brontë to Genêt.

"Where in Heaven's name were you?"

"We had pudding!"

I think that this declaration will bring me the benevolence accorded a solemn confession. But there is no absolution, and certainly no indulgence, from the furious mother. As for the father, he is still splitting his sides with laughter before Madame Roberge, who chooses to leave this site of contradictions before she loses her mind. I don't know what to do to calm Maman's expression, which reminds me all of a sudden of Nurse Sirois's diabolic look. I tell myself that if Truth would give these fine people a slap, things would be back in order. But she doesn't appear. I think about the Bittèlzes on the radio who made me so happy. I tell myself that my sadness equals theirs and that they're my last hope for communicating with my mother, who has started to howl with rage. I start to sing in English, the language of sadness.

> *Love, love mi doux*
> *You no aille love you,*
> *Al alouèse bi troue,*
> *So pliiiiiiiise! Love mi doux!*

Sometimes talents are born that go unnoticed, divine gifts that stay hidden forever because no trigger brings them to the light of day. At that moment, I discover that I have a gift for languages and for making people laugh. Maman's sobs stop after just one verse of the pathetic threnody from England and my father finishes collapsing in the rocking chair with his ultimate spasm of laughter. He manages to wheeze,

"They were at Boubou Pizza!" I will use that God-given gift
for the rest of my days. Also, I realize that English makes
absolutely no sense. If those lowdown blues can't make my
mother sad — even though she's on the verge of a nervous
breakdown, and they are being sung in the language of
the damned who can't understand French or maple syrup —
it's because there must be deep rifts in their idiom. It's true,
she's won over by a laugh that begins with little spasms.
"Don't you ever go there again!" and "I thought you were
dead!" are transformed into shudders that are nasal and
absolutely deafening. Truth will have to shed some light on
this English that's more and more mysterious.

The happy family scene ends with the departure of my
father, who must have some thief to chase, and with a feast
of caramel cake. Maman understands: if she doesn't want
her progeny to hang around the sleazy streets of Amqui,
taking sugar from the first person they meet, she'll have to
be a little more generous. Each of us then draws a lesson
from Truth's valuable advice. I will be eternally grateful to
my sister for taking me along on this rewarding adventure
and to my father with his cop's radio for giving me my first
English lesson. We'll never go back to Boubou Pizza alone
or in company. Boubou will fold some years after our visit.
In my memory, though, it will always be my first trip — the
beginning of the true odyssey of sweetness that will take
me from Amqui's maple syrup to West Indian molasses to
the tortes of Upper Austria. The journey to the pizzeria also

contains the seed of all the heartbreaks I will live through in airports and railway platforms; like a prophecy, it announces the pain of departures and the greatest pain of all: the return of one who comes back speaking languages that his people don't understand. I believe I can hear the snickering of ugly Truth from the bottom of the river — unless it's a salmon giving up its last air bubbles before dying in the place where it was born, after a journey to the Atlantic.

෴

IN THE SUMMER OF 1973 I get all the sugar I want from my mother. Still frightened at the prospect of an illicit excursion to Amqui, she seems resolved to supply me in order to keep me away from what she sees as dangerous: the waitresses at Boubou's, boulevard Saint-Benoît and the Hells Angels. Once again I spend some very happy hours in our garden, serving tea to Minou and introducing Moussette to English. Our pooch is making noteworthy progress. My most enjoyable hours, though, are spent with Truth, who persists in appearing only to me. Her nakedness, she claims, would make the adults feel awkward.

"I heard about your little escapade. Congratulations — you made your mother nearly die of sorrow."

"I was following your advice!"

"You mustn't get caught, you idiot! Next time, don't stay away so long. And get it into your head that sugar isn't everything in life."

"I don't see how someone who lives naked in a river all year long can afford to give me that kind of advice. Don't you ever go out?"

"My travelling days are over. I've learned now what I wanted to."

"Are you going to spare me all the dangers of the grand boulevards and betray my secret?"

"It's not a secret. You have to go out and come back. That's all. The rest is philosophy. It's something you'll learn in due course."

"You aren't being very explicit ..."

"Fine. Okay. Very well, so be it. The journey itself doesn't matter. It's where you go that matters."

"Whew! That's reassuring. As recently as yesterday I heard Papa say the very opposite."

"Some day he'll learn, too. I travelled for a long time before I ended up here."

"Where did you go?"

"Paris, India and Estonia."

"Did you like it?"

"It was fantastic. But enough idle chitchat. Today I want to talk to you about a danger greater than boulevard Saint-Benoît — greater for you, that is. Nothing can touch me."

I've had enough sermons about boulevard Saint-Benoît to understand that Truth isn't fooling around. The comparison with the boulevard is not insignificant. A danger worse than that? Maman was clear though: nothing is more dangerous for me than one of those cars racing down the road at top speed. What could she be talking about?

"Your neighbour …"

"Madame Roberge?"

"No, not the one across the street, she's an ally. She'd keep you in sugar even after your mother's death, though I don't really approve. I'm talking about your next-door neighbour, Madame Loignon. Let me show you …"

She leads me to a house that, despite its proximity, has never been the object of my attention. It must give off very bad vibes if it escaped my frenzied research during my attacks of withdrawal the summer before. Indeed, I have to accept the fact that this house is a vortex of evil, the lair of the Beast: Madame Loignon. The Loignons' property is separated from ours by a garage on piles and a dense row of willows. Moussette and Minou sometimes go there, but I'm not brave enough. And for a very good reason! What Truth shows me that day is worthy of a horror film. Behind the hedge and under the harsh Canadian sun stretches, as far as the eye can see, what she explains to me is a vegetable garden. Very straight rows of low plants, all of the same height, have been planted there by an obviously baleful spirit.

"What's that?"

"Vegetables. Very close to us you'll see turnips and, after that, potatoes, carrots, and — at the very end, under those long green stems — the hiding place for big round onions."

✆

SO MANY DESCRIPTIONS, SO many monsters, so many screams. A scene in an excellent horror film captures better than anything what I'm feeling at this very moment. Only science fiction has the power to present the intense disgust that will always make me shudder. In *Aliens* — the sequel to *Alien* — the heroine, Ripley, is shipped back almost forcibly to the planet that her crew had visited in the first film. It was on this planet that her crew had made the inopportune discovery of some horrible creatures with two sets of jaws that kill on sight and have a generally nasty disposition. These parasites from outer space have an appallingly complex reproductive cycle: first, the queen lays pumpkin-sized eggs in a warm spot. The eggs then wait for a human, before hatching to produce a yellowish octopus that attaches itself to the face of the victim and deposits a deadly foetus in their ribcage. After a gestation period, the foetus bursts out violently from the unfortunate victim's chest, killing them after some atrocious convulsions. The brilliant process will make a fortune for the producers of this disturbing work. In the sequel to the first film, Ripley is horrified to discover the queen laying her murderous eggs, and so she gives them a treatment with a flamethrower. The scene is heartbreaking: the queen howls in pain at the sight of her progeny burned to ash. We could, however, debate the underlying motives for Ripley's acts — I've neglected to say that the foul creatures have already decimated her crew, and that she is trying to keep the bugs from falling into the hands of the wicked military. You can't be too careful.

When she went back to the cursed planet, Ripley knew pretty well what awaited her. But in my bucolic Canadian Eden I could never have imagined that, at fewer than twenty metres away, the root of all evil is growing with impunity. Images of mashed food and goose-stepping nurses file past before my eyes. So that's where they come from. Is it possible that so much evil can grow on my plateau, in my town, nearly under my nose? Brilliant ploy. So the alpha of suffering has been lying in wait for me ever since my birth. Next door to me the Doctor of the dark hospital stocks up. The devil is always closer than we think — it's classic. The murderer is always someone known to the victim — that's a truth worthy of Hercule Poirot. Truth has ducked out, too. Once again she leaves me with a dilemma. It happens that at my age I've not yet seen *Aliens* and, even if I were given the chance, where would I unearth the life-saving flamethrower? I go home, sick at heart. Once again, help comes from Marie-Josée.

☙❧

"VEGETABLES COME FROM THE neighbour."

"What?"

Marie-Josée is obviously shaken by that unassailable revelation. Of the two of us and the Roberge children, it's hard to say who hates mashed vegetables more zealously.

"They stretch out as far as the eye can see. Turnips, potatoes, carrots, and ... and onions!"

The last-named, with their slimy texture when cooked, make us shudder in horror at their mere mention. We are convinced that cooked onions are converted into worms by an inexplicable process of sublimation. We decide to call the Roberge children to our rescue; after all, it's in their interest as well as ours to deal with the problem. We have to involve them; the number of vegetables is most certainly too great for us on our own. We conclude that the adults must be left outside the plot, along with Nelly Labelle, the other neighbour across the way, a notorious sneak we suspect of spying for Madame Loignon. A plan is drawn up, worthy of the FBI. Like Ripley, we aim at the total and complete annihilation of the vegetable garden. Our reasoning is simple but the greatest military victories have been won thanks to disarmingly simple ideas: Japan's surrender was not obtained until Hiroshima and Nagasaki were annihilated; Paris was conquered by simply passing through Belgium; Germany was conquered by quite simply opening two fronts simultaneously, proof that military strategy is not a matter for philosophers and mathematicians. If it were, the number of human wars could be counted on the fingers of one hand. I come, I see, I conquer, and meanwhile I destroy. We are confident that once the vegetables have disappeared, an elementary economic principle would be set in motion. The reasoning is this: the offer of vegetables having been reduced to zero, producers will have to turn to acceptable substitutes, namely maple sugar and puddings. Marketing will do the rest, and consumer preference will quickly reorient the markets. Do we fear a sharp price rise caused by an abrupt increase in the demand for sugar? It's possible, but the market will deal quickly with that temporary problem: the country is covered with maple trees.

We take advantage of an evening when our parents have gone out to move onto the attack. Absent-minded Valérie is back at work and everything is set to call on the troops to carry out the plan. It's a question of hiding under the garage on piles and taking advantage of the darkness to uproot the baleful plants. Eight hands won't suffice to finish the job in one go, and a number of raids will prove necessary to wipe out all the crops, but there's no question of giving up before we begin. The perfidious Loignon notices nothing. The vegetables, once they're pulled out, are piled into foul-smelling heaps under the garage and left there to rot. I work away furiously on the unfortunate onions with particularly fierce determination, while my sister and our two acolytes attend to the turnips and the carrots respectively. The potatoes cause a particular problem — once the leaves are pulled off, the tubers do not follow. They stay deviously underground, like a mutant virus that has learned how to lie low in new depths before the onslaught of drugs. We have to put off their destruction until later. Over several days we slowly work away at the evil garden. The Augean Stables were not cleaned with more determination and zeal.

❧❧

ONE NIGHT, WHEN WE plan to continue our work of destruction, little Nelly Labelle, the Roberges' neighbour, ventures silently under the garage and discovers our diabolical plan. We hadn't expected to be discovered like this — we had taken great care to attack just as old lady Loignon was going inside after watering her vegetable garden.

"What are you doing?"

"Mind your own beeswax."

"I'll tell!"

"We'll kill you!"

The traitor disappears before we have time to bribe her with candy. Later, we will find out from her mother that she's crazy about vegetables. You can't be too careful.

The job has to be done before Nelly sounds the alarm. In a suicide operation we dash into the vegetable garden, yanking out whatever we find — until, like a she-wolf whose cubs have been stolen, old lady Loignon appears in her garden along with Nelly Labelle, who is pointing a cowardly finger at us. Caught red-handed "de-vegetablizing," we take refuge under the garage. The rest falls under the Nuremberg Laws. The discovery; the appeal to the shrew for help; the alert given to my father; the taking of the garage; and the discovery of our piles of vegetables in an advanced state of putrefaction. The punishment will be legendary. No refrain by the Bittèlzes will subdue the general anger. I don't understand a thing.

Confiscation and prohibitions, sermons and deprivation,

mark the end of the summer of 1973. The failure of our plan is all the harder to swallow because we have to help old lady Loignon harvest her ghastly now-ripe vegetables, and she gives my father a ton of carrots and turnips. I learn a new sense of anticipation, close to happiness, that is called the desire for revenge. Indeed, I swear that the Labelle creature won't get off so lightly and that she'll be punished. We swear, all four of us, that we will have no rest until she has paid and paid dearly for her betrayal.

6

THE LITTLE BITCH LIVES in a house adjacent to the Roberges', at the top of a very steep iron staircase. In the winter we have often seen Nelly's mother putting salt on the steps to prevent her little ones from breaking their necks on their way down to the yard. Revenge is a dish best served cold. In Amqui, if you wait for a few months, it's possible to serve it frozen.

The piles of vegetables have been more or less disposed of from under the garage by Papa. But as he is too big to slip into the small dark space, he has made very quick work of it and left behind some nice juicy onions. In October, at the time of the first wintry days, when Truth appears to me with her skin tinted slightly blue by the cold, I decide to take my revenge in the name of all those I love. Very early one morning, I arrive before anyone who lives on the plateau and retrieve one of the decomposing onions. Once broken in two, the whitish sphere lets out some worms, the only creatures worthy of such a habitat. The rest isn't for the faint of heart.

I creep up the Labelle's staircase and leave my nightmare onion on a step. I go back down, hidden behind a maple on the Robergs' property, which is now ablaze with the colours of autumn. I wait in the morning cold. After a good while I think for a moment that my plan is too simple — old lady Labelle will come out and see the rotten bulb. But there is a god for addicts.

Nelly is the first to emerge from the residence. As is her habit, she hurls herself down the stairs to start her informer's day. Who is she targeting today? It hardly matters. My stratagem, as malicious as it is effective, will rid her of her taste for attacking us, permanently. Her foot slips on the rot with a sticky sound. Her screams rip through the morning as her little body hits the metal steps. Her scrawny vegetarian's skeleton makes dry cracking sounds that warm my soul on this cold October morning. Crack! Right femur! Let that be a lesson, you tedious little brat! Creak! Left ulna! You'll need a lot more! Crack! Right radius! How are you going to point your finger now? Creak! Four spareribs, four! Hindenburg lands on the icy concrete. Cries of pain.

When she hits the ground the whole neighbourhood is awakened. From all sides, people come running to rescue the bitch. I watch the scene from under my maple tree: the tearful mother who is trying to grab the urchin, screaming in pain, "Where did that onion come from?" Madame Roberge with her head in her hands. The Roberge children laughing their heads off on their balcony. It's all my work. Suddenly the sky confirms the sanctity of my venture. Heavy snowflakes start the winter of 1973–1974 just as the paramedics are rolling the stretcher with the traitor aboard. The first snow blesses this morning of revenge with a thin white coat. I reveal myself behind the trunk of the maple tree so that Nelly can see me, so that before she leaves for several weeks in the hospital she can catch the image of my happy face trying to swallow snowflakes which I still think of as soft, frosted gifts from the sky over Amqui. When she sees me she stops shouting, strangely freed by knowing why her pain has struck. She knows that the next time will be fatal. Revenge is complete. Nelly has the right to an extended hospital stay, to the fine care of the Doctor and his Nurses. Suspicions will hang over my person for a long time because of that rotten onion, eloquent evidence that bears my signature. Doubt is allowed to remain, probably out of fear of the scandalous appearance of Truth. At the end, I gain some new suppliers: old lady Labelle and old lady Loignon, whether from fear or pity, have started offering me sweet things. How hard is it to understand? If Nelly cares about living on the plateau she has to submit to certain rules. There's no question of tolerating such bad behaviour.

7

THAT WAS WHEN THINGS became clear in my mind, a mind already devastated by the ravages of sugar. All that adversity, all those efforts deployed in vain to limit my access to the divine substance confirm just one thing: that sugar is the reason for living, an end in itself — and to that end I will devote the rest of my existence. The events that follow this observation will compete to reinforce my obstinacy. First of all, the arrival of a new character in my microcosm confirms my vocation as enemy of President Nixon. It heralds Operation Glucose '74, which will precipitate the fall of the sugar thieves. With the appearance of Adrien, my schemer's qualities will transform the entire population of Amqui into an invincible army fighting for full and absolute domination of the world. Nelly's fall down the stairs has led to the sudden appearance in our lives of a new character whose influence I won't understand until much later in my life. When the little devil landed at the bottom of the stairs with a thump, a pudgy bald man emerged from the main floor of the Labelles' house to rescue the shrew. I'd never seen him. I ask Truth:

"Who's the bald man?"

"A bachelor."

"What's that?"

"He doesn't have anyone he can give his sugar to."

"That opens some prospects."

"Be careful! People in the neighbourhood are wary of him."

"Why?"

"Absolutely no reason. Out of simple meanness and envy. He makes wonderful kites children adore."

"Can I have one?"

"First you have to sweet-talk him, become his friend — and, by the way, breaking your neighbours' bones isn't the way to make friends."

"It's the result that counts. The kid won't rat on us when the neighbour gives us candy and she'll avoid me. I win on all fronts."

"Mmm … I've got a friend called Morality… an acquaintance, I should say. I wonder what she'd have to say about it."

But I've stopped listening, already thinking about the bachelor. How is it that on this street, where there's no shortage of kids, an adult can't get rid of his sugar? I'd like to make it a winter project. I can put my own shoes on now and get dressed to brave the cold winds outside. I've decided to make Baldy into a new supplier by summer.

One morning, I head straight for his place. Incredible luck — he's shovelling the freshly fallen snow off his balcony. I plunk myself behind him so as to size up this enigmatic character. For a long time he makes as if he doesn't notice I'm there. I'll start with a little withdrawal crisis, I think. I feel my heart beating faster and I'm perspiring despite the biting cold. I have to break the ice.

"It's cold."

"Hello little boy. What's your name?"

"Eric."

"You're the policeman's son?"

"Yes. What's your name?"

"Adrien without an H. What can I do for you?"

"Can I see your kites?"

The question puzzles him.

"It's not really the season. But if you want to see them, you have to come inside. And, if I let you inside your parents will start a fight with me."

"Why? Are you a thief?"

He's definitely no good at being cross-examined.

"No."

"So I don't see the problem. All I want is to see your kites."

"If you promise not to tell a soul, come in!"

So Adrien invites me into his den. I immediately regret
the oath he made me swear, because what I see is worthy of
Europe's greatest museums. He lives alone in a big apartment
full of bright colours, where all the walls are hung with
paintings that depict fields of unknown plants, beets, maps
of tropical islands and other strange images. He is a curator
in the Sugar Museum.

"What are all those pictures?"

"Fields of sugar cane."

"Cane?"

"Sugar comes from sugar cane. Don't you know that?"

"Where are those canes?"

"In the south, the West Indies, Cuba, Jamaica; it doesn't
grow here."

"So sugar ..."

"Yes, it comes from the south."

I'm knocked out. How could people hide such an important fact from me? I was born in the wrong country. My
whole existence hangs on the cultivation of those long
tropical plants. Adrien explains the history of sugar. If he
is to be believed, sugar has been the reason for wars, for
deporting entire peoples, for colonization and massacres.
He emphasizes some place names that sound strange: Carib-
bean, America, Egypt, New World.

"And beets? What are they for?"

I am surprised that an earthy root from the row of potatoes has a place in this divine collection.

"The Germans were the first to discover that you could produce sugar from a beet. There's no difference between that sugar and the sugar we eat."

"Germans are geniuses."

"Umm … in chemistry, it's true. But make no mistake: the history of sugar is not for the tender-hearted. The propagation of sugar cane in the West Indies opened one of the darkest chapters in colonial history: the slave trade. The boats that took the sugar to Europe went back to the New World laden with African slaves taken away by force."

"How could the Europeans eat something like that, covered in blood?" The question struck me as very relevant just then.

"They've always been crazy about it. As far back as the Middle Ages, it was recommended for treating fear, anger and bad moods."

For treating fear, anger and bad moods. What I thought I'd discovered in Amqui, Europeans had been practising for centuries. Against fear, anger and bad moods: sugar.

"I should tell you the story of chocolate, coffee and diamonds … No, come and see my kites."

Along with pictures on the history of sugar, there are kites hanging from the ceiling of his apartment, which covers the whole main floor. Some are fairly primitive, lozenge-shaped; others depict cats, dragons, insects. On the low table in his living room sits a crystal bowl filled with multicoloured jujubes. I'm dying to ask for some, but I don't know what he might want in return. I let him set out the rules for our deal. He doesn't make me wait too long. He takes me by the hand to his cellar. I'm trembling with apprehension. He starts to talk volubly about all sorts of things, especially his do-it-yourself projects. He shows me his work bench, his tools and his projects under construction. One attracts my attention. This aerodynamics genius has undertaken to depict Truth on a kite. Does she know? How did he meet her?

"That's Truth! You really got her right!"

"Thank you."

The compliment wins me two jujubes. After that, I just have to listen to him and I get access to what seems to me a bottomless supply of sweets. He must have been stockpiling them for a long time. He talks and talks and talks. I look at him, wide-eyed. When I've had my fill, he invites me to leave and reminds me solemnly of my vow of silence. That silence will weigh hard on me for a long time, but I admit that the prospect of losing such an easy source helps keep me silent. With him, I just have to listen and ask questions. Which comes to me very easily.

I go back to Adrien's at least twice a week. He's started to vary his inventory of sweets just for me. With every visit I learn a little more about kites. He shows me photos of models that he's sold for a small fortune. Every time I go home, however, after lying about where I've been, I feel something like dissatisfaction. I find the vow of silence hard to bear. It's as if Marco Polo had been forced to be silent under pain of death about the wonders he had seen in Asia. My dependence on Adrien's sugar dictates silence to me, while the wonder of all that I've seen and heard at his place demands an audience. Truth hardly visits me anymore since Nelly's accident and I feel terribly lonely. Why is life like that, why must the sweetest delights be kept secret under pain of having them taken away?

As well as his kites and his countless chocolates and other sweets, Adrien owns the complete collection of the Bittèlzes. First, he teaches me that they are four in number and, then, the meaning of their songs in French. To my amazement, their rhymes laud not sadness but outlandish things like weeks with eight days, yellow submarines, Norwegian woodlands and I don't know what else. Closer to madness than to suicide.

That's not all; he often calls on me when he is constructing his kites. I become an apprentice artistic advisor, helping him now to make Truth more lifelike, now to choose the colours for a flying fish that he's making to order for a wealthy lady in Amqui. Sometimes I nearly forget about the candies. He always reminds me. Unlike all the other suppliers in the past, he suggests them; I don't have to beg and worry about losing them. That paradise lasts for at least three months. In a word, it lasts as long as Nelly Labelle's convalescence. In the winter of 1974 I feel my first genuine urge to strangle someone with my bare hands.

☙❧

I HAVE NEVER BEEN good at silence — I rant and rave against everything. If I'd been in Allende's secret service, Pinochet's torturers would have had an easy time. It will take me years to understand that some things can be said and others are best kept to oneself and even longer to organize what I know into the two categories. My visits to Adrien are becoming an exception, though — I make a conscious effort not to talk about them in front of anybody. Several reasons justify this self-censorship: first of all, I mustn't say a word about the existence of this new supplier to the other children, including my own sister, lest the stock of sugar dry up too quickly. I am becoming a skinflint with age. Second, the other suppliers mustn't learn of the existence of this new competitor, simply to avoid destructive rivalries and the formation of a collusive oligopoly that would cause an inflation in prices. Third, I don't mention it to Minou or Moussette for the plain and simple reason that my new friend confessed to me that, to his great shame, he is violently allergic to my two faithful animals.

ତ୍ଧ୍ର

NELLY LABELLE GOT A hospital sentence that would make any American prosecutor pale with envy — she was back in the vicinity around Christmas. Once again the proximity of good and evil strikes me as an illogical but necessary rapprochement. December brought to all the suppliers — Maman, Madame Roberge, Madame Loignon, Madame

Labelle and other neighbours — an abundance heretofore unseen. Sugar flows freely on the plateau, and it's not worth bothering to stock up for slack days. In all the houses, monuments to sugar have been put up and decorated with shiny balls, little angels, stars and garlands. As in the Garden of Eden, one need only reach out a hand to pick from the conifer branches a chocolate or a piece of marzipan. It was a question of seeing who would make the most cookies, fruitcakes and marmalades. At the height of this period, comparable to the Roaring Twenties, comes the Woodstock of sugar: Christmas. It is explained to me that the day marks the birth of our Saviour Jesus Christ, conceived by the Holy Ghost, born of the Virgin Mary, suffered under Pontius Pilate and founded a group, probably something like the Ells, to spread the good news. The celebration of his birthday, though slightly repetitive, is a pretext for everyone to close their eyes to an overconsumption of sugar. Adrien doesn't shy away from these rituals and has the nicest Christmas tree on all of rue Saint-Louis. Making the most of his kite-making talents, he has produced a tree that is frighteningly beautiful. I seem to be the only child with the privilege of permission to come close to it. My awe before his creation fills him with joy.

One day when I come home from one of my secret visits to Adrien, I want to impress my family with the latest knowledge he has taught me.

"Today, from fifty to sixty per cent of all industrially

manufactured foods contain sugar, whether or not we can taste it. Sugar is an integral part of our diet."

"Where did you pick that up?"

"Umm … from the radio; they were talking about it this morning. And the purer the sugar, the more of it mankind has eaten."

"You're living proof of that."

"It takes a ton of sugar cane to make three hundred pounds of sugar."

To impress my father, I disappear into my room for a few moments and then come out with my version of a sugar cane in green crayon.

"And you heard that on the radio too?"

"Umm … no, I saw that on TV!" (Lying comes naturally to me today.)

Making my father fall for a special radio program about sugar is one thing. Hoping that all the networks have declared a national sugar week is something else. One detail escaped me: we don't have a TV. Not until a week later will it be installed in the living room at the request of my mother who is bored to death. The first image broadcast is a close-up of President Nixon.

"Why is he so ugly?"

"Sssh!"

Before me stands the antithesis of Truth. I shudder.

The fractured little neighbour was discharged from the hospital a few days before Christmas. The frail little bundle of bones has slowly mended, but a cruel tonsillitis had given the Doctor a pretext to keep her in his camp longer. She comes home, then, two glands lighter and various casts on various limbs heavier. Still, she manages to stroll from the top of her metal staircase to the bottom despite her mother's ban. As if driven by an innate instinct for spying, she catches me going into the lion's den in search of a bell-shaped chocolate. I haven't been at my supplier's for five minutes when the wretched little traitor knocks on his door three times. Adrien, to my great displeasure, welcomes her like a queen. She looks at me out of the corner of her eye while savouring some green marzipan, and greets me with words that have double and triple meanings that only I can understand. "Bonjour" has become, in her mouth, "Gotcha, you little bastard!" Anxious cramps wrench my guts.

What has to happen happens: the little bug informs her mother of my presence at Adrien's; the woman tells Madame Roberge who, not realizing that she has some classified information, spills the beans to my mother. Nelly Labelle, whom I thought I'd destroyed, has come back like the creature in *Alien*, stronger and meaner than ever. I have no doubt that she personifies evil on this earth, but I'll always wonder why and how that sad vilification had to happen around Christmas, the sacred feast of sugar. Bad karma? Lousy destiny? It had a strong smell of vegetables.

Other mysteries surrounding the Adrien incident will never be cleared up; I will die not knowing what really happened. First of all, it seems clear to me that my mother doesn't play fair. There were other suppliers in the past — Solange, Madame Roberge, Boubou's waitresses and others who escape me. But Maman is livid. Usually she wouldn't have breathed a word to my father and would have simply reminded me of loyalty. This time there's a confab, visits in uniform to Adrien and questioning à la Miss Marple.

"How long have you been going there?" (Mind your own business.)

"Why didn't you tell us?" (To avoid this kind of hysteria, actually.)

"What did he do to you?" (He did me a lot of good.)

Is it clumsy of me to say: "He's very nice, he showed me his kite and his tools. Then, in exchange, he gives me chocolates."

Truth wouldn't have done a better job of silencing them. For a long time there will be a deathly silence in the apartment, interspersed with oaths and sobs unsuccessfully held back. A court is deftly improvised at which everyone except Truth is invited to testify. The instruction gives as much importance to my testimony as it would to the statement of a bum. Interestingly, the main accused, my bald supplier, is never brought in for questioning. It's as if at Nuremberg they had merely listened to the victims without trying to corroborate their accusations with the responses of the Nazis. This case is slightly different insofar as the crime committed doesn't appear in the criminal code. The putrid and foul-smelling Nelly Labelle, rattling along on her last cast, is even invited to give her version of the facts.

"But she goes there herself!"

I try to incriminate her; there's no way that I'm going to hell on my own. Even if it means confessing my near-murder in October, I am prepared to drag her into this sordid matter. But justice doesn't deign to adjust her scales just now. No one sees anything at all reprehensible in the fact that Nelly also stocks up at Adrien's. She who has always feigned purity, who swallowed her foul vegetables in silence, stuffs her face at her neighbour's and I'm the one who takes the rap. I have to go back to preparing a smaller dose of sugar for myself. Once again, the shakes, my nerves in a knot; the only support I get is in the warmth of Minou and Moussette. I'm more than ripe for a frank discussion with Truth. Before my sentence is even handed down, I sit in the yard to await her visit.

"What's this circus all about? Why the clamour, the questions?"

"You've infringed a thousand prohibitions at once. You really can't be trusted. You're becoming a danger for everyone you approach. I myself am beginning to fear for my safety."

"You? Wouldn't that take the cake! You only put in an appearance to criticize or to drag me into doing something stupid. I don't want to see you anymore. Go and advise Nelly if I'm not a worthy disciple of your school of thought!"

Truth doesn't flinch. She tells me that she's used to being dismissed by everyone; indeed, she is very surprised that our relationship has lasted so long. To tell the truth, I'm beginning to find her nakedness a tiny bit vulgar. Her habit of criticizing me after the outing to Boubou's, the ransacking of the vegetable garden and my visits to the bald man leave me stunned. Did she not more or less openly lead me into each of those adventures? Has she not very often been the snake in our earthly paradise? So far, she's been a very mediocre advisor. I'd have been better off listening only to my bad instincts and going on with my little life without letting her intervene. She's beginning to look ugly.

"Besides, you're a scary sight."

"Any more shocking revelations?"

What happens next marks what any Freudian psychologist seeks often in vain in his clients: the precise moment when the shock occurs. The initial trauma. Truth, in all her ugliness, raises above her head her streaming wet whip, and deals me a blow on the left side of my face that I'll feel again when I see the painting by Gérôme.

"With that, I leave you. Think about it."

No need to think it over. The pain shoots through my skin to the bone. It's my cries that make my mother come running into the snow-covered garden.

"What happened to you?"

"Truth hurt me!"

Had I told her: "O rage! O despair! O inimical old age!

Have I then lived so long only for this disgrace?" she'd have given me the same smile.

Maman had blamed this inept reasoning on a nervous shock picked up at Baldy's. She drags me inside.

୧୦

CHRISTMAS COMES AND GOES, and it's February again. According to the Roberge children, Nelly Labelle still visits Adrien every day. Injustice is flagrant then, but people ignore it; it glides yellowish down our walls. Truth no longer comes to see me, Marie-Josée is totally weaned off sugar, and I am alone, sticking like a forgotten turnip to the bottom of a kettle of loneliness. How can it be that some can shed their habits simply by thinking about something else while others, like me, seem condemned to a life of torture? I'll never know. I will meet people who at some point in their lives will find themselves reduced to the state of human wrecks after abusing cannabis, vile powders, Dutch chemicals or sports. Some will be able to extricate themselves from their mire by thinking one fine morning: "Enough!" They will resume a normal existence by throwing themselves body and soul into an exhausting job, or else get jobs with the federal government. Others will follow detox treatments that will be more or less long, depending on their means or the means of their welfare state. No guide to sugar detox will be written. I'll go on waiting.

Marie-Josée turned around before she'd reached the point

of no return. I, for my part, persist in finding new suppliers at the risk of sacrificing Maman, Truth and whatever time in Paradise I still have left. I am trying to follow Marie-Josée this winter. If she has found peace without sugar, I should be able to also. Once again I have to put myself in her hands.

8

"SOON YOU'LL CELEBRATE YOUR fourth birthday."

That's Truth. I haven't seen her since our last quarrel. I'm ecstatic to see her after so long.

"Where were you? I looked all over!"

"You and everyone else. I took a little vacation under the ice. I prefer to space out my visits, it makes me more desirable."

"You haven't changed."

"You have. I don't know if I approve. You've grown thin. If you were a few years older, I would say that you have a broken heart ... Anyway, that will come soon enough."

"I hardly eat any sugar now. My only supplier is Maman and even so ... You'll understand, after the incident at ..."

This is new. When I try to say Baldy's name, and Nelly's

betrayal darts through my mind, my throat tightens so that no sound can get through. That feeling of suffocation is usually followed by tears and, even though I'm so sociable, by a strange desire to be alone. This time, Truth holds me gently to her and I smell the pleasant freshness of her skin on my cheek, which reminds me of the icy softness of the bark of maple trees in winter. With her long hair she dries my tears, and, for the first time, I have the impression that the tone of her voice is more tender. She, who usually lets every word fall like the blow of an axe, is making a conscious effort, I think, to speak more softly. She appears to me again like the one of whom I want to ask a thousand questions.

"Did I steal something?"

"No."

"So why were they all so upset when they found out I was getting cookies from Baldy?"

"You wouldn't believe it."

"I wish I understood!"

"So does he. Anyway, today we have to look toward the future. In fact, that's the main reason I'm here."

"Now what? Are you going to tell me to kill my sister? Set fire to the house?"

"What I have to tell you is a little tricky."

When Truth starts a piece of news like this, it's best to lie low. It's as if Etna started to tremble, saying, "Oh my, I think I'm going to have a little gas tonight ..." Enough to wipe out Sicily's peace of mind. Truth is in the habit of slapping without warning, of striking without being detected on radar, and now she makes an announcement. I'm expecting the worst.

"You're going to move."

"Excuse me?"

"You-are-go-ing-to-move. That means leave Amqui. And go somewhere else."

She might just as well have told me that Minou and Moussette had taken up bridge! I begin to explore the various possibilities of this move. She was, of course, very careful to reveal only what was most painful. To move: according to my first fantasy: the entire plateau, including houses, neighbours, cats, friends, enemies, baldies, family, Roberges and long-hairs will be located in a new place that's bold enough to have another name. After that, my imagination draws up scenarios that are more and more appalling. The move includes just my house and the garden, plus the cat and the dog. The prospect fills me with horror. If my present situation only lets me get sugar from my mother, what will it be like in the new place? I imagine for a second; just one second, because my young mind can't tolerate the thought any longer. The new place will be inhabited by people who only speak English. I picture myself strolling through a crowd of long-haired Bittèlzes, trying to make myself understood during an attack of sugar withdrawal. What will become of us? Another possibility, this one absolutely preposterous, comes to mind: that just me, Marie-Josée,

Papa and Maman are going to leave, without the cat and the dog, taking with us only the green Ford. I don't realize it, but I'm fantasizing like a prisoner of war, imagining the most incongruous, unbelievable situation so that I won't be disappointed whatever the real outcome is.

Once the abomination has been accepted and nearly digested, I have the very human reflex of looking for a guilty party. Who is responsible for this terrible disturbance?

"Why?"

"Your parents have decided."

"Without consulting me?"

"As with most things … All right, I just wanted to let you know. Know how to go away."

"What do you mean? When will it happen?"

"I think they've decided on August."

"And why are they waiting to tell us?"

"They're afraid of your reaction."

Afraid of my reaction? Is it possible that I once inspired fear? At a certain time then, people feared me. Later on, I won't be spared like that. Which is why childhood is a golden age. They fear you, they spare you, they don white gloves. Then things change for the worse. The respect that's shown me will be inversely proportional to my age. Decades later, the same announcement will be served up by my mother with no psychological preparation. She'll simply toss off, between two chitchat sessions, "We're moving." I imagine that in ten more years she will neglect to inform me at all, and that I'll find out when I pay her a surprise visit and realize that her apartment has been invaded by total strangers. This certainty — that age will bring only contempt and negligence — I acquire at the age of three. I shudder at the thought of those old folks to whom no one says much anymore, who are treated like furniture. "We're going to put you there, gramps, then you'll be able to see outside ..." The age of three will only fill me, for a while, with the certainty that I no longer matter for anything or anyone.

And so I await the official announcement of the move, and I've decided to use it as a weapon for getting more sugar. The news is a long time coming. I decide to force Maman to spit it out.

"Maman, what does it mean *to move?*" Subtlety has never been my strong point.

"Who told you?"

"I don't know. What's *to move?*"

I expect a definition that will confirm my most optimistic anxieties, the ones where half the town will follow us in our exodus.

"It means to change your house or your town."

"House? Are we nomads?"

"Yes. Since you seem to know, we'll be moving in August."

"Who with?" I ask, aghast.

"What do you mean who with? You, me, Marie-Josée and Papa, that's all."

At that I start to shake. What do you mutter then, wretched Pythia? What priestess will translate your horrible gurgling into coherent information? Would you try then to tell me that the rest goes without saying? Or do you intend to tell me that you will wrench me away from this blessed plateau and travel to some cursed lands? Do you know at least what you're doing to me?

"I don't want to."

Condescending laugh.

"I won't go. Why do we have to? What did we do?"

"Nothing. Your father's been transferred."

Transferred. That term will be with me throughout my childhood, like a curse. My father's sad job obliges him not only to run after thieves, it also forces him to change towns once all the thieves in the first town have been caught. They'll spring that on us I don't know how many times later. Between the ages of one and sixteen I will move no fewer than ten times. That means an average of 1.2 years per house. Our stay on rue Saint-Louis was relatively eternal. After Papa's transfers, there will be all sorts of reasons to throw my sister and me out of one home and into the next, and we'll learn quickly not to ask any questions when a move approaches. In fact, in a short time we will become experts at moving. Some children are forced to take lessons in piano, ballet, gymnastics or other disciplines from a very young age. We are trained in moving. At sixteen we will both be Masters in Moving, Doctors in Farewells, virtuosi in adapting to new surroundings. Few can say that. But the announcement of the first move affects me the way the Acadian deportation in 1755 did Baie Sainte-Marie.

"Why aren't the neighbours coming with us?"

"Because they're staying here!"

"And the cat? And the dog?"

"We'll see."

"Why is Papa transferred? Aren't there any more thieves?"

"That's it. He has to catch thieves somewhere else."

"If there aren't any thieves in Amqui, why is he never at home?"

Dense and heavy silence.

"We'll have a birthday party for you in June. You'll be able to tell everybody goodbye."

I imagine a meal along the lines of the Last Supper. This move is giving me anxiety cramps. They're going to ship me off to the unknown and that last party will be my last chance to pick up enough sugar for the journey, to bring together all my suppliers in the same place to extract something from them to survive on.

9

ALONG COMES JUNE, THEN, with its lilacs, warm breezes and my last birthday in Amqui before we leave for somewhere else. I didn't even ask where we were going. To me it's all the same. Do people on their deathbeds ask the doctors where they're going? Is the soldier on the railway platform in a war movie informed of his final destination? The goal of our journey can't be interesting. It can only be a no-place, a place without sugar, filled with tears. When you want a verdant oasis, in every direction lies the lethal desert of sand strewn with the skeletons of camels and reckless travellers. One morning, though, I will get some clarification as to the goal of our journey.

ᎧᎧ

SOME MORNINGS BELONG TO US, to me and my sister. One of our favourite activities is to haunt the kitchen while our parents are still asleep and to search the cupboards for sweets. My sister, who has climbed onto the counter by who-knows-what monkey's trick, bombards me with what she takes from the cupboards. Sometimes she sprays me with any white powder she finds, so that one morning my mother finds me sitting in the kitchen, covered from head to toe with white powder that Marie-Josée probably thought was icing sugar. Amused by the scene, she'd photographed the bombardment. That photograph will be around for a long time. When people look at it they will recognize joy on the face of a girl who thought she'd discovered a magical cure, and disappointment on the face of a boy who's tasted a foul substance that he thought was sugar. Some addicts know they've been had after the first line of coke. The photograph shows the premonitory face of that disappointment.

On that June morning, instead of haunting the kitchen we lay siege to the garden. Our parents think that we're still in our bedroom and they talk very loudly, loudly enough so that we can hear them in the garden through the open kitchen window.

"It's definite then? We're going back to Rivière-du-Loup? You've got the job?"

"Looks like it."

"What do you mean, 'Looks like it?' Have you got it or not?"

"Yes, yes, we're going. You can tell the kids."

"They already know."

"How can they?"

"You know what they're like, there's no way to hide the truth from them. Just last week they were asking about it again."

"Well, they'll have to get used to it."

"It suits me fine."

"Of course it suits you! You're the one who made me ask for the transfer."

"Listen. Unless you get me out of here, I'm leaving."

"Don't get mad, it'll all be over in August."

"If she follows us, there'll be hell to pay."

"She'll stay here."

So they sealed the bitch's fate. I knew that her carefree nature would ruin her one day. She wasn't going to follow us. She must have barked too much in the middle of the night once too often, or dumped a pile in a corner or engaged in some other obnoxious behaviour that was her ruin. But I'd been suspecting this foul, horrible, disgusting abandonment ever since my conversation with Maman, so I'm not shocked. My sister, though, is petrified — this conversation has turned her into a pillar of salt. Like me, she doesn't like the name "Rivière-du-Loup" at all. So we're to be wrenched away from our earthly paradise to brave some wolves at their river? It's no surprise that they're being careful to leave the cat and dog behind — the wolf would polish them off in no time. But us? What will become of us in this adventure? Will there be people in these places to protect us from the wolf that's so big its name has been given to a river? Tears flow.

"Marie-Josée, stop teasing your brother!"

Usual unwillingness to understand.

10

THE ATMOSPHERE IS HEAVY in our little family. Papa is away more and more — something about catching the last thieves who've taken root in Amqui before we leave — and Maman throws herself body and soul into preparations for my fourth birthday. My sister and I have discussions that seem like confessions of the damned. I always initiate these exchanges with a question full of anxiety.

"Do you think the wolf will eat us as soon as we get there?"

"You're judging him a little fast. Maybe he's a vegetarian."

"But what if he has a bad history?"

"Then maybe we should take advantage of life right now."

"Meaning?"

"Forget your good resolutions and eat all the sugar you can get your hands on."

It's during one of these morbid interrogations that the death of Moussette is announced. We learn quite bluntly that a crazy truck flattened her as she was crossing rue Saint-Louis. My first bereavement. I go through all the stages of acceptance of the poor creature's death and I demand, like the families of plane-crash victims, to be taken to the site of the tragedy. Strangely, no trace of the smashed beloved canine is visible. It's suspicious. We heard neither squealing brakes nor lamentations. When did it happen? Papa and Maman give contradictory versions of the mass-acre. One of us finds out that the truck was red, the other that it was black. I was dying to see Truth emerge from her river to shed a little light on this sombre story.

At first, the neighbours seem to know nothing, but a few days later they corroborate the facts as related by Maman. Moussette is no more. I realize that Maman quickly tires of the questions we ask her, and I'm left with a mystery. Why, I will always wonder, are the great mysteries of child-hood always those on which we want to shed light at any price? Some years later, I will compare the dog's death with those of JFK or Elvis Presley. The last two will leave me cold, but those three deaths are the bases of the most elaborate conspiracy theories that exist. Was it possible that Moussette, unbeknownst to all, ran away after hearing about the move and is wandering around Amqui in search of a new abode? Or could she have been the victim of Nelly Labelle's thirst for revenge? Did she throw the dog into the sewer system? I get bogged down in conjectures. I'm sure that my parents' account is a tissue of lies and that some day the gallant canine will reappear and astonish everyone. Like Elvis's fans, I will wait forever after. Even when she is thirty years old.

The disappearance of Moussette, no matter what the exact circumstances, can only exacerbate our fear of the wolf. Either she has been sacrificed so as to be saved from a more painful death in the jaws of the beast, or she refused that dark fate of her own initiative. With no more explanations, Maman serves up a story that deserves to be told.

"Where's Moussette?"

Exasperated sigh.

"She's with Jesus."

"The same Jesus we celebrate at Christmas?"

"Yes, right, Baby Jesus. He lives in Heaven with God."

"God who?"

"God ... Umm ... God God!"

"Hasn't he got a last name?"

"No!"

"Like Cher?"

"Right."

"Who is Jesus?"

"He's the Son of God. He came down to earth to save mankind. He has a beard."

"Like the Ells?"

"Hardly."

"Does he save bitches too?"

"Yes, that's why he took Moussette."

"Did he steal her?"

"No! No!"

"Because if he did Papa will catch him, for sure!"

"Please, go and play with your sister."

Maman slips me a cake and ships me outside. She is sad these days; Moussette's death must be gnawing at her, too. So there's a thief running around in this town who "saves" men and bitches, and whom my father hasn't gotten his claws on yet. It won't be long. Two years later, I will learn through audiovisual miracles that Jesus is not little at all, although he really does have a beard. His beard won't be at all like the Hells Angels' beards, round and lush. You could have called it a shaggy mass of hair that must be infested with lice — he didn't take care of it. He wandered around barefoot — something strictly forbidden to us for obvious climatic reasons — in hot dry lands, followed by a noisy crowd that demanded miracles from him. His picture confirms my doubts: he really does look like a dog thief. For a long time he will be the prime suspect in Moussette's disappearance. I hope that he'll come back and take Nelly Labelle, the Doctor and Madame Loignon with him to Heaven.

11

JUNE. THE WONDERFUL MONTH of June in Amqui, bathed in the soft light of the northern summer solstice. This month always brings its share of sweet things, like sugaring season and December. Maman has made sure that our time in Amqui won't go unnoticed. With the aim of conversion she created my birthday — the celebration consists of winning more aficionados of sugar every year. Like Celtic witches, she chose a date coinciding with the summer solstice to emphasize the cosmic superiority of glucose and its benefits to the individual. The ritual cannot do without an enormous cake, which is sacrificed to be passed around to all the guests, young and old, who will repeat the exercise once they're home.

꙰

OUR LAST LAST SUPPER in Amqui assembles the most important suppliers on the plateau: Madame Roberge, Madame Loignon, Solange, their respective husbands, their brats — they've even declared an armistice so the little Labelle girl can take part in the celebration. New suppliers are initiated too. I think that it is due to Maman's efforts that Nixon finally loses the war against an enemy he hadn't sized up properly. Holy Communion with sugar is gaining in popularity because, around the huge table set up in the garden, there is talk about other birthdays for which our celebration will serve as a model. Madame Roberge will do the same thing for her children after we leave, inviting new neighbours who will make the custom universal. I'm sure that even the Doctor must have succumbed to these new practices but never realized it. The epicentre of this sweet upheaval is Maman: the Joan of Arc of glucose.

My fourth birthday is starting to resemble the Carnival in Rio. Even under torture I couldn't list all the guests. What is certain, though, is that they'll all go home and perpetuate for their kinfolk what they've witnessed in our garden. This memorable day will provide forever the sweetest and liveliest memory of the battle with the anti-sugar forces. My mother gained ground at top speed. The one who shines by his absence from this celebration is my father, which is a terrible shame because the fireman dropped in and even gave me a miniature red fire engine.

"The truck is from Madame Roberge," says Maman

hesitantly. The neighbour shoots her a knowing look.

"No it isn't! The fireman brought it and I saw him!"

My mother takes me aside and I don't know if it's what she said or the fact that she interrupted my sampling of the holy cake that left me more perplexed.

"The fireman never came. The truck is from Madame Roberge. Okay?"

Through the willows I can see Truth with her head in her hands. For the first time I choose to look away from her to concentrate on what the others want to see.

"Understood."

Truth avoids me until the blue car shows up.

ℭℛℴ

A FEW DAYS AFTER my birthday, I'm hanging around the garden with the Roberge children and my sister when an uproar comes to us from inside. Someone is sharply opposed to someone else. Cries, tears — in two words, indescribable chaos. For a moment I think that the wolf can't wait for our arrival and has decided to attack the plateau. My sister and I go inside briefly just to see. In their bedroom, my parents are playing some unknown game. My father is piling clothes into a suitcase open on the bed while my mother is emptying it. The little game goes on with more and more frantic movements. It seems forbidden to talk during this game. The winner must be the one who manages to close the suitcase which is either completely empty or full to bursting.

My father takes the lead, but Maman discovers an infallible move: as soon as the suitcase is half-full she turns it upside down so that the contents fall out. Is that manoeuvre allowed? Is it cheating? My sister is following the match, wide-eyed. I imagine that later on we'll try the new game of speed and skill in our room.

"What are they playing?"

"I don't know."

Maman strikes me for the first time as a bad loser. Indeed, since Papa was able to fill the suitcase and then close it, she throws herself onto the bed, pounding the pillows with both fists. But the game is not over; now a second, even bigger suitcase has to be filled. Everything goes in: socks, pants, police uniforms, cap, shoes, shirts, undershirts, in total disorder. I think to myself that if Baldy had been able to play this confusing game, he'd have probably been careful to meticulously fold everything he put into the suitcase. His mania for perfection, which was expressed so clearly in his kites, would probably have assured Maman of an easy victory. My father, very familiar with the race, has the advantage of speed. I'll never know how Papa wins the suitcase game; Marie-Josée drags me outside first. There, I ask the other children for the name of this new sport.

"What are they doing?"

"Divorcing," replies one commentator.

"Will it last long?"

"No, just as long as it takes to leave, that's all."

"Why are they divorcing?"

"Because they aren't in love any more."

The expert's answer perplexes me. *In love?* What's that? And if they aren't in love any more it must mean that they were before, regardless of what that implied. I wonder if I could play the suitcase game even though I haven't been in love. The phrase strikes me as feeble; it lacks consonants. It is pronounced half-heartedly, without needing any great conviction. It's not like *chocolate*, a word that implies the entire phonetic mechanism, or *cake*, that forces gutturals and dentals into a happy marriage. *In love* seems capable of being transmitted by accident, while asleep.

Overcome by deep and total boredom I leave the group of children, who have decided to wait for the outcome of the match outside the apartment door. I've never been a sports fan and this game bores me as much as a cricket match. Climbing the steps from the garden to our parking space, I notice a small blue car parked there. A visitor? Someone to admire the divorce match? Behind the wheel, none other than the dreaded Nurse Sirois smiles at me.

Galvanized by my edifying dialogues with Truth, armed with the gift of speech, this time I know how to chase her away. It's something like when the doctor asks you to describe a pain in your head. You know that you've never experienced it before, but it hurts in the same place. And so you use the first pain as a yardstick for all those you will experience in the same place. It's the same kind of unpleasant reconciliation that makes me study the strange woman with my big eyes.

"Bonjour."

The blond smiles.

"Is everything all right?"

"Yes."

My suspicions are well founded. She has the same snappy tone as the Nurse. I tell myself that she must work in the health care sector, too, and that she must know what it means to be in love. I go up to her and say: "You know, my father isn't in love with my mother any more ..." I don't have time to go on; her tight smile melts like snow in the sun. She doesn't make eye contact, as though I had just said, "Out of here in the next twenty seconds or I'll chop you into pieces."

With a few jerky movements she cranks her little Japanese car and disappears down rue Saint-Louis while Madame Roberge looks on, wide-eyed. She didn't give me time to complete my question. I was intending to ask her in to watch the divorce match, but she took fright it would seem. I go back towards the garden. I notice that Truth observed the whole scene and has been giving me a knowing look. My father won the match and is coming out of the house right now, a suitcase in either hand. He walks to the parking area, stops, studies at length the space left empty by the blond, then turns around and goes back.

Never again will I have a chance to attend another divorce

match. Maman, a poor loser by nature, will refuse to play. As for me, I'll never learn how.

Oddly enough, after that incident, Truth never appears to me again. Her presence won't be pointed out anywhere. She won't even honour me with a farewell. I realize quickly that it's easy for me to forget her. Her absence from my life removes the heavy burden of always having to talk about her. It is at that moment that Fiction, her cousin who is all made up and wearing a sequinned evening gown, makes her entrance in the film of my existence, to everyone's relief. Yes, I confess, she is more presentable than the cantankerous swimmer.

12

JULY BRINGS, ALONG WITH its heat, the ideal opportunity
to proceed with Operation Glucose '74. The summer of
the condemned people passes at lightning speed. We sense
the approaching deadline for our move while imagining
that, at the last moment, a divine force will come and cancel
the journey towards death. Maman and Papa have a happy-
go-lucky attitude that drives me crazy. From the ghettos
of Eastern Europe during World War Two, valuable testi-
monies on the existence of people doomed to die shed light
on the feelings that have haunted me in recent weeks. It
seems that the Jews confined within old cities behaved as
if their lives would be spared. The news that came to them
from outside would have destroyed the morale of the greatest
of optimists: the Germans had graves dug outside the towns

and cities. They were intended to become the receptacle for their carnage. In those ghettos, people knew that the graves existed because they'd been dug by their people. Despite the signs carved in Gothic script in the Ukrainian sky, people went on with their daily lives. Some knit scarves for winter, others gave French lessons to children who wouldn't live another week. The end of the world had been announced, but routine continued to rule people's existences. My departure would not come until I had settled accounts with the sugar thieves once and for all. To carry out this diabolical plan I would need the help of all my allies.

I explain the plan in detail to Marie-Josée, who seems more alarmed at the consequences of a defeat than at the glory of a total victory. She agrees, with bad grace, to help me. She certainly owes me that. To achieve my last mission in this land I just need two or three tins of maple syrup. No way of unearthing them at our house; the product was banished long ago. Adrien, though, has some stock in his cupboards that he doesn't know what to do with. It's a question of taking them from him. If he knew my ultimate goal, he would give it to me; but it's best not to compromise him in this plot that will mark forever the future of humankind. Though I've been forbidden to visit my kite-maker, I take advantage of my parents' absence to knock at his door. Marie-Josée has been given clear directives: at the signal she is to sweep into the kitchen, grab three tins of syrup, leave as fast as she can and hide them under the garage. Entering Baldy's den proves to be very difficult.

"You know very well that your parents don't want you to come here."

"Yes, but you know that we're moving in a month and I haven't seen Truth's kite finished."

"What if you got caught here? We'd be in a fine mess."

"It will just take a minute, my parents are out ... We go down to the basement, we come back up, and that's it!"

He sighs, hesitates, then lets me in without locking the door, as I was hoping. My sister is spying on our moves from the window. As soon as we're in the cellar, I hear her creeping in. I spend a good five minutes with Baldy, asking him a thousand meaningless questions to give my acolyte a chance to accomplish her deed. When I decide that she's had ample time to complete her mission I leave poor Baldy, who is barely starting to be interesting.

Marie-Josée is hidden in our room, panting, eyes bulging.

"They were heavy!"

"Get ready for worse tonight. We have to take them to the hospital."

"Why?"

"You'll see. I can't say too much."

That night I don't sleep a wink. Outside, the hot July night has plunged all the inhabitants of the plateau into sleep. All I have left is to hope that the rest of my plan unfolds without a hitch. My sister doesn't let herself be pulled out of sleep without a struggle. There's nothing worse than a sleeping child. I have to pinch her till she bleeds to make her open her eyes.

"Time."

"You're out of your mind!"

"Get moving, out the window!"

I am dragging the three tins of maple syrup around like a time bomb in a backpack borrowed from the Roberge children. The alarm clock in our bedroom shows one o'clock. The cornerstone of my plan is still missing. Tugging the sleeper by her hand, I begin to hope that everything will unfold as planned. Going down rue Rodrigue, I see him. He is there as promised, the biker who pulled me out of the garbage can and whom I threatened to expose to the official police unless he obeyed my orders. Because in the meantime I realized that bikers are scared to death of visits from the official police. If Solange ever testified about our motorcycle rides ... At noon I didn't give him a choice: "Be there at a quarter after one, with your bike." And he's there. His mission is very simple. He is to take us to the hospital where the rest of my diabolical plan will come to an end. The biker complies and in five minutes we have come to the cursed place. The rest could have come from James Bond.

There we are, right in the middle of the deserted hospital's parking area. Its darkness freezes us in dread.

"How do we get in now?"

"Trust me."

I have no idea what road to follow. We go around the main door and end up behind the enormous building. There, a black door lets in rays of light. From inside, voices and kitchen sounds break the heavy silence of the valley. Suddenly, the door opens wide to let through an enormous lady holding a green bag in either hand. She leaves the door open and disappears into the dark towards some huge garbage cans.

"Let's go!"

We end up in a vast, deserted kitchen. So this is where the Doctor's revolting brews are cooked up. The fat lady's footsteps come closer. Hidden behind a gigantic counter, we watch her switch off all the lights, put on her coat and leave. In the darkness, lit up by the stainless steel of some tremendous fridges, the kitchen from hell is all mine.

"Open a can of syrup, fast!"

My sister complies. Each fridge contains an enormous kettle half-full of different mashed vegetables. Each one gives off a nauseating toilet smell. Into the smelliest I empty a whole tin of syrup and, using a spoon that Marie-Josée has unearthed, I recompose the mixture. Deciding that we've done what we can in the kitchen, we sneak down a deserted corridor lined with closed doors and with an elevator at the end.

"We'll get caught! Let's go home! I'm scared!"

"We can't, the kitchen door shut behind us."

⊘⊘

WE HAVE TO DO something. Marie-Josée calls the elevator. The sugar god brings it up empty. I press 1. We emerge into a barely lit corridor where we can hear, coming from several doors, *beeps* and the laments of some patient suffering from sugar withdrawal. During my stay in the thousandth circle of hell I noticed that, unless a patient wakes up in pain, visits by night nurses are rare. We don't risk getting caught. A deathly silence reigns over the hospital, broken only by the snap of a can opener. Marie-Josée still understands nothing and trembles like a leaf at the thought of being discovered in these places of suffering by a Doctor or a Nurse.

"Can you see the people in the rooms?"

"Yes."

"We have very little time. Climb onto each table in silence. Don't worry, they're drugged, and you pour a little syrup into the water bag that's attached to their arms by a tube."

"What for?"

"You can ask questions later, we have to be out of here before one o'clock. Hurry up."

And that is how every sleeping patient in the Amqui hospital receives in his IV that night one liquid ounce of blond syrup. We carry out our plan without being disturbed by the Nurses, whom we've learned to avoid. On the first floor, the geriatric wing lets us develop a muffled way of walking that doesn't disturb the old people's light sleep. In Oncology, patients confuse us with chemo-induced hallucinations. In the nursery, the lips of each infant are sealed with sugar. On the top floor we find patients without IVs pacing as they talk to themselves. They would sow panic in anyone, but observing them carefully shows that there is a hermetically sealed aura around them that keeps us from entering their world. Their senses are inaccessible to us. Ignoring us completely, in their delirium they swallow the final ounces of syrup. We can guess from their hollow eyes that our furtive image won't survive the dawn; we have nothing to fear from their memory that is forever dead. In any case, no one would give the slightest importance to their incomprehensible gibberish.

Hospitals are made in such a way that it's easy for a child to hide under a bed, behind a door, in a closet and so forth. After an hour of relentless effort, we've gotten rid of our whole stock of sugar. The empty tins are tossed into a garbage can where, thanks to the Doctors' maniacal cleanliness, the evidence is guaranteed to disappear in the morning. I've studied my gulag carefully. It is when we are leaving via the fire escape that fate grabs us by the ankles. We hear someone tripping lightly up the stairs. Terror paralyzes us. An immense shadow appears now just above the landing. We're going to be caught. No place to hide, no garbage can in which to disappear. We close our eyes, convinced that a Doctor or Nurse Sirois is going to cut us into little pieces.

"Look at that! The cop's kid!"

I recognize the voice right away. It's my angel, Notre-Dame-de-l'Espérance, coming up with a pile of clean sheets.

"What on earth are you doing here at this time of night?"

After the scene with the fire engine, I've found out that Truth can't bear to be brandished in front of everyone.

"We were visiting Madame Loignon and we fell asleep and we're looking for the exit."

"And your parents? Surely you didn't come here by yourselves!"

"The policeman's waiting for me outside." This is only a half-lie as we will note less than two minutes later.

"Tell your Papa that visiting hours are over at nine o'clock!"

"Yes, Madame ..."

In less time than it takes to say *heart attack*, we're outside in the parking lot.

"Now, how do we get home?"

The question is a major one. How indeed are we going to travel the kilometres separating us from our abode before dawn? There again, the strategic genius I've inherited from my mother saves us: the biker is waiting for us as I'd ordered. A parallel policeman, as I should have explained to Notre-Dame-de-l'Espérance. Without a word, he helps us mount his steed and drops us off next to the candy trailer, grim-looking in the moonlight.

Five minutes later, we are back in our beds. While we

sleep, my revenge drips little by little into the veins of the Doctor's patients who will never understand why Madame Viens woke up in the morning with a big grin, though she'd just lost her appendix, asking for bread and jam. For his part, that morning Monsieur Tremblay, an abstemious and moderate man, adds three sugars to his coffee. Madame Perrault, grey from a long night's sleep after a painful delivery, wakes up at a flick of the whip of Truth. In the Doctor's unspeakable prison, a series of addictions young and old are born. My sister and I have been careful above all not to miss any of the children sleeping in the wing reserved for them. Worried mothers find their offspring, usually so calm in the morning, gritting their teeth and demanding a soft caramel. Operation Glucose '74 turns out to be a monster success, and constitutes the epicentre of the influence of sugar in the town, the province and even beyond our boundaries. At that moment, Richard Nixon, still fast asleep in the United States, feels a twinge, something like a tingling at the level of his liver. He turns over and goes on sleeping.

ℭℽↄ

A FEW DAYS LATER, my mother is surprised to learn that the markets in Amqui have been stormed by entire families from the region. Shelves are cleared of cookies, pastries assaulted, there are fights over ice cream, macaroons, cakes, brown sugar and other forms of glucose that are now necessary for the mental survival of the population. No one can explain this phenomenon. Those who were in the hospital during the night of our action impose on their families a diet high in sugars of every kind. Even stranger, patients in the hospital delight in mashed turnips and noisily demand extra helpings. The demand is so great that Solange must replenish her stock of sweets. But the most satisfying victory, the dish that crowns this brilliant scheme, is the sight of our neighbour Madame Loignon replacing her vegetables with flowers. The rows of carrots, turnips, potatoes and cabbage become lovely flowerbeds with petunias, roses and gladioli. We spy on her through the hedge. She sings as she finishes digging up a foul onion, holding a bit of chocolate that she nibbles now and then when she takes a break. As of that day, one woman will refuse to give me the smallest sweet.

.

13

THOSE MONTHS OF FIERY passions also have an effect on certain inhabitants of the plateau. As I will learn much later, heat waves are uncommon in these far-off parts of Canada. The town of Amqui is situated in the heart of the Gaspé peninsula, a region swept by winds from every direction. Near the shores it is surprising when the North Wind doesn't blow, so much so that a decision will be made to put up a windmill in a few years. It hardly ever happens that this isolated part of the east experiences the scorching heat characteristic of other parts of Canada; every time the mercury goes above twenty-five degrees, the horrified population draws an *x* on the calendar to mark the event. Amqui experiences a very different climatic reality. Protected from the sea winds by the Appalachians, the small town becomes an oven in July. The extreme temperature has consequences for everyone. You have to be motionless, seek the shade, and avoid any overly violent exertion. On some days, the suffocating heat makes already fragile individuals lose their minds. It will happen to Nelly Labelle who will be the victim of an unfortunate heatstroke.

☙

MARIE-JOSÉE HAS RESUMED contact with Nelly who, since my birthday, hasn't been bugging us. She has been seen stuffing her face with every kind of sugar. People claim they've seen her revelling in maple sugar at Baldy's place; she has held onto him as a supplier. But, one day during the hot spell, baleful spirits that were slumbering in her waken and cry vengeance for the abuse we subjected her to in the past. Possessed by hatred and bitterness, she pushes my sister down the iron staircase that leads to her residence. The Roberges and I are witnesses as Marie-Josée glides, then lands on the ground with a thud. A sick smile adorns Nelly's face. Her efforts are in vain: Marie-Josée doesn't have a scratch. All right, the surprise takes her breath away and we have to pick her up and lay her on the Roberges' sofa; but she comes round in two minutes to the great displeasure of Nelly, who thought she was taking revenge for the attack of which she was victim last fall. What disappointment on her face when she sees my sister get up from the sofa and walk! "Witches!" she must be thinking. Indeed, she is dealing with magic. I remove her from her torpor by biting her hand with all my might. She has to be wakened. It takes three people to pry my jaws from her tender flesh. Nelly disappears in the direction of her abode and we hear nothing about her for at least two days. Apparently her mother got carried away, brought her daughter to Maman and showed her the clear marks left by my teeth.

"Your son bit my daughter!"

"How can you be sure she didn't start it?"

"That's no excuse."

"He won't do it again."

What my mother meant was: "He won't have to do it again." Indeed, the terror in Nelly's eyes confirms that she has now understood that she will never touch us, that her attempts at destruction are doomed to fail.

I realize that we've finally won the sugar war. All the neighbours, without exception, are now aware of the virtues of the glorious substance, and the influence of our victory will dash the plans of the Doctor and his Nurses. As the silent victor in this war, that will in fact last some three years, I will keep until today my personal confidences about the fall of the sugar thieves. As today marks the thirtieth anniversary of that night of the full moon when my sister and I fought against the plans of the sinister Doctor, I consider that the time has come for Truth to appear in the open. Where are you, my magnificent drowned woman?

14

ON THE MORNING OF August 9, 1974, my parents did the unthinkable: they got up before we did.

"How come you're up?"

I was used to enjoying a few moments alone in the kitchen with my sister before they got up.

"We're moving today."

We're flabbergasted. So the Last Judgement is here. Big strapping fellows empty the house of its contents and fill a truck. My parents watch.

Later on, years later, I will be horrified to read *The Diary of Anne Frank*, *For Those I Loved*, *Holocaust* and other stories filled with sadness about the deportation of Jewish people to the camps. While I am reading, I will have a sense of déjà vu. I will never be able to put my finger on the feeling of confidence that lets people allow total strangers to strip them of all their possessions.

"What are they doing?"

"Helping us move. We're taking all the furniture to Rivière-du-Loup."

The wolf won't be content with our tender flesh, he'll also need our sofa, chairs and dessert forks. Minou must have sensed this great disturbance and taken refuge somewhere else. Gallant cat. Apparently when the North Sea dikes burst on February 1, 1953, canaries had anticipated the deadly flooding of Zeeland. They panicked, hitting their heads against the bars of their cages, trying to warn their owners of the imminent calamity. Our Minou, by deserting as he's done, followed his instinct. His mysterious disappearance corroborates my worst anxieties. The cunning feline smelled from afar the breath of the wolf that will devour me. But like the happy-go-lucky Dutch, my parents didn't know how to read the warning sign from the animal kingdom.

The truck is full, the house is empty. Only the television set still has pride of place in the living room because my mother has declared that it's too fragile to be entrusted to the movers. It is when I'm alone in this room that I experience an epiphany. I have learned how to make images appear by pulling on the green button. I want to do it one last time, certain that the image box will stay behind with everything that has mattered to me so far. After a muffled sound and some time to warm up, the wan face of President Nixon takes shape on the screen. His complexion is even paler than when he first appeared; ugliness possesses it entirely and a blue-tinged hand, streaming wet and icy, holds him by the neck. He stares at me for a long time and introduces me on this morning of our move to the face of defeat. I listen attentively to the French translation of the words of this human wreck. At that moment, I know that I can die. I leave the house and, to everyone's surprise, I settle of my own accord on the back seat of the green Ford, waiting to be handed over alive to the wolf.

❧

THE STRAPPING MOVERS PUT everything they have into the move. Our sacrificial procession will travel by night to the den of the beast. Madame Roberge and her brats say their farewells as in a film by Oliver Stone.

"You'll come back and see us!"

"Yes, we promise."

"Farewell, darlings."

God knows why the only thing I can think of to say at that moment is: "Nixon's gone, now they need a Ford."

Blank looks.

Even little Labelle gives us a kiss. *Morituri te salutant.* I can't even look her in the eye, so badly do I feel like crying. The Ford turns onto rue Rodrigue. At the bottom of the hill, Solange waves at us. Standing on the back seat, I stare for the last time at the plateau where I was happy. What I see there seems to me, even today in my dreams, a vision. High in the sky the wind is holding up a kite depicting Truth. Adrien wanted to say goodbye, and this is the ingenious way he's devised. The car drives onto boulevard Saint-Benoît. For a long time I will watch as the kite shrinks then disappears behind the maple tree. We pass Boubou's. I realize then that for four years I've been the victim of an optical illusion. The city ends right after the restaurant. At first I think that we are driving through a vast park, but no, we've left Amqui in less than five minutes. How can it be? From our plateau, the city seemed infinite. All that time we thought that we had lived in a metropolis — but now it is revealed in all its insignificance. Here there are only meadows, forests and peaceful cows along the road. We drive onto a long, steep hill. I can see that Amqui is actually tiny; it fits into my little hand. It looks like a heap of little sugars in the Matapedia Valley. At the bottom of the hill, a small blue car also turns onto the hill that leads towards the river of the wolf.

I fall asleep, exhausted from sorrow.

And in the morning, the big bad wolf won't eat me.